THE HOMES

THE
HOMES

J.B. MYLET

First published in Great Britain in 2022 by
VIPER, part of Serpent's Tail,
an imprint of Profile Books Ltd
29 Cloth Fair
London
ECIA 7JQ
www.serpentstail.com

Copyright © James Mylet, 2022

1 3 5 7 9 10 8 6 4 2

Typeset in Garamond by MacGuru Ltd
Printed and bound in Great Britain by
Clays Ltd, Elcograf S.p.A.

A CIP catalogue record for this book is available from the British Library.

ISBN 978 1 78816 704 8
eISBN 978 1 78283 805 0
Audio ISBN 978 1 80081 057 0

FSC
www.fsc.org
MIX
Paper from
responsible sources
FSC® C018072

For Alice and her gran

1

'*Les!*' whispers Jonesy from her bed. 'Lesley, you awake?
I cannae sleep.' This time louder.

'*You* cannae sleep? I'm the one whit's got to fight her.'

'I know, I cannae sleep, you're gonnae gub her.'

'Nuh-uh, I'm deid, I'm so deid.'

I haven't opened my eyes yet. I know if I open my eyes
I will have to be awake and if I am awake it's morning,
and if it's morning I'm going to have to fight her before
school starts and she's twice my size.

She is Glenda McAdam. I hate her. I didn't start
hating her. She's always hated me. I did nothing to
make her hate me; I wasn't horrible to her, I didn't
say nothing about her, but she just always hated me. I
think it's because when I was in the same class as her,
I was always top. She didn't like that. I'm not in the
same class as her now, I've not even been in the same
school as her since last August. There's one school at
the Homes for most of the kids, but me and three
others – one girl and two boys, all of them older than

me – have to get the bus and train every morning to the grammar school.

The fight is at 7.30 a.m. My bus comes at 8 a.m. The fight is outside the front gates, where the paths meet the road into the Homes. Glenda's cottage is only fifty yards from the gate. The cottage me and Jonesy live in is on the hill and looks down towards the gate. You can see Glenda's home from ours. When I finally make myself open my eyes, I see Jonesy has her head at the window. She's watching, staring at Glenda's cottage for signs of action.

Glenda McAdam is a bully. She's my bully, but she bullies everyone else too. She's got friends, but they are only her friends because they are scared of her. I am scared of her, but I'm not willing to be her friend to avoid it.

I shouldn't have agreed to the fight, but I was the one that suggested it. Glenda's always picking on me, has done for years. So I told Jonesy I was going to fight her, and that I thought if I fought her it would make her stop picking on me. Now I think I'd rather she just continued picking on me.

'She's gonnae bust my heid, Jonesy. She could kill me.'

'She's no gonnae bust your heid. She's gonnae hit you a bit and make you say you give up, but then it will be done. And if you're lucky she'll leave you alone. Mibbie let her hit you a bit and start greetin'.'

'I'm no greetin, I'm gonnae get a knife.'

'You're no gonnae get a knife.'

'I am, too.'

'If you stab her, her brothers will get you. If you just let her win then she'll leave you alone. Pretend to try at the start, then let her win. She's gonnae win anyway, so just let her. You're making a sacrifice. It's a smart move, Lesley, and you're the smart one. Lose the fight and the big hippo will leave you alone for ever. If you're lucky, you could get in there and smash her one before she gets hold of you. Just don't let her sit on you. She's a beastie, that one; if she sits on you, you're definitely deid. I've seen her sit on her friend before and her friend went blue.'

'Can't I say sorry?'

'Nah, you can't back out now, everyone's coming. You back out now and everyone will hate you. You said fight, and if there was no fight they'll all want to fight you for denying them a fight. Those are the rules.'

'I feel sick.'

'Course you do, I would too. Still, it'll be over soon and then you'll be fine.' She looks at the clothes I laid out on my chair last night. 'Do you want to pack another school shirt?'

'Why?'

'Cos that one's gonnae get blood on it and they're no going to let you get away with that in your school.'

'Aw no, I like this shirt. I'll wear something else for the fight, a rubbish one.'

'Are you really going to do it?' comes the voice from the bunk at the end. It belongs to Shona. We share the room with her, Eldrey, Pam and Mary. Eldrey and Shona have the bunk beds at the end. Shona's bed is the one on top. She says as she's the oldest she should get it. She's the eldest by three days.

'Aye,' I say, trying to sound confident.

'She's gonnae gub yuh,' Shona says.

'Aye,' I say, fully aware of what is going to happen.

'Good luck,' she says. 'And if you can, kick her in the fanny, if you can find it on the big monster.'

Jonesy laughs.

I would laugh too if I wasn't so scared.

*

We wash our faces in the sinks and I get dressed. I wear my normal skirt but I wear my shirt from yesterday as it's going to need a wash anyway.

I wonder what Glenda McAdam is doing now. I bet she's punching the walls in preparation, eating raw eggs and getting into a pure rage.

Jonesy goes down to get some breakfast, but I go back to my bed and lie on it. I can't eat, there's no point, plus everyone else in the house is going to be staring at me, they all know about the fight. I think our houseparents, Mr and Mrs Paterson, know about it too. They are not going to stop it, either. She'll be helping Cook lay out the plates for breakfast; he'll be sat reading the paper with everyone tiptoeing around trying not to annoy him.

Jonesy comes up after her breakfast. She's brought me toast. She leaves it on the floor by my bed.

'It'll be all right, Lesley, you'll see.'

It won't. But it will be over, and all I care about is it being over. I've just got to get through it, and I don't want to greet. Not in front of Glenda or in front of anybody.

4

'Right,' I say, 'I'm ready.'

I don't feel ready. I'm never going to be ready for this. I feel so sick. It's time to leave the cottage. No amount of wishing is going to get me out of this. I've got to just do it.

I get up, leave our bedroom, and walk down the stairs, Jonesy following behind me. Everyone is watching. Everyone knows this fight is going to happen.

As I leave, no one says any words of encouragement. They know there's no point. They know I'm finished.

Mr and Mrs Paterson don't try to stop me. Fights are going to happen, they can't do anything to stop them, so they don't.

Is this what boys have to go through every time they have a fight? Then again, they just start fighting, they're not stupid enough to pre-arrange it and make themselves sick with worry waiting for it to happen.

I walk down the path and I'm shaking. I've never felt so ill.

I see Mr Sharples, the caretaker. He sees me, he probably knows what's going on, too. He's not going to stop it either. I can tell by the way he is looking at me that he knows I am in for a beating and is just going to let it happen.

There's twenty kids at the gate already, boys and girls together, all excited to see me get hurt, and I realise it's not just Jonesy who's followed me out of the house – all of them are here, joining the crowd. I've done nothing to them, but then sometimes anything here that's a break from the normal is what gets them excited.

People like seeing other people get hurt. Humans are cruel.

I pace back and forth by the entrance gate; if I stand still they will see me shaking. I want to cry. I am not going to cry. I want to run away. I want to be anywhere on this planet apart from here and now.

I can see Glenda McAdam's house, Cottage 8; there's people waiting outside it. I keep looking to see if she's coming.

Her brothers are waiting; her brothers are even worse than her. Her whole family is Gorbals feral, her older brothers are some of the maddest people in here, they're pure crazy.

I could get out of it by begging. As long as I'm humiliated, this can be over. But I'm tired of her, I'm tired of the grief.

'There she is,' says someone behind me, and a surge of nausea sweeps over me. I thought I was feeling sick before, but this is worse.

Glenda is coming out of her cottage. I want to run away and never come back.

'Be calm, Les,' says Jonesy.

I could charge at her? Take the fight to her, go on the attack?

But I don't, I can't. I stand on the spot, frozen.

She's coming. She's big. She's so big. And ugly. Oh, Christ.

I feel the blood rush to my face. My muscles lock up. I clench my jaw.

I keep my spot, by the gate.

The gate.

I can see her face. I can see her nostrils flaring.

She's coming.

She's saying something. She's shouting at me.

I can't hear what she's saying.

The gate!

Ready?

BANG!

Just as Glenda gets to me I grab the gate and swing it, swing it with everything I've got, and it hits her.

She goes down.

She's down and she's groaning, and I don't know what to do.

I'm standing over her.

'HIT HER!' they're shouting.

'HIT HER! KICK HER!'

I grab Glenda's hair and pull her head back, but I don't hit her. She looks stunned.

I lean down, my hands still shaking, and I say, 'Please leave me alone.'

There's blood on her head. Some runs into her eye. She's confused. 'All right,' she says.

'Promise?'

'I promise,' she says.

I let go, and then walk off towards the bus stop. There's a groan of disappointment from the crowd. The kids wanted more fighting. They wanted more pain. Some of them are following me. Someone shouts, 'Wooooo!' It's Jonesy. Others are cheering too.

Jonesy jumps on my back. I glance back and Glenda's

still on the floor; her little cronies are trying to help her up.

I still feel sick. I'm still shaking. Oh God, I hope it's over now.

I start to cry. I didn't want to cry but I can't help it.

Jonesy holds me tight while I sob. Some of the others around me start patting my back. I want them to leave me alone, I just want to get on the bus. I pull away from Jonesy, then I'm sick on the grass. The kids around me are laughing. This is their entertainment for the day.

'Can you leave me alone now, please?' I ask.

'Yeah, leave her alone,' echoes Jonesy.

They do what she says.

She walks with me to the bus stop, holding my hand and squeezing it tight.

'You knew you were going to do that, didn't you? The gate. You knew all along. God, you're so clever. You lured her to that spot and then *bam*!'

I don't say anything. I don't because I don't want to lie.

I didn't have any plan for the gate. I didn't have any idea what I was going to do. It wasn't until she was stood in front of me that second that the idea came to me.

I get to the bus stop to see the bus coming down the hill.

'Hey,' Jonesy says, squeezing my hand again. 'Hey.'

I look up at her. She wipes some of the tears from my face.

'Lesley Beaton,' she says, 'you're my hero.'

2

I was put in the Homes when I was three weeks old.

The Homes is an orphans' village. It was built at the end of the last century as a place to put all the homeless children from Glasgow. There are about thirty cottages and nearly eight hundred children, and each cottage has a housemother and housefather, plus a cook. It's a self-contained place with its own school, church, shops and even a small hospital.

Us kids aren't necessarily here because our parents have died. Lots of children are like me, put here because we couldn't be raised by our families.

Some of us were taken from our parents for our own safety, as they weren't capable of looking after us. If the mother died sometimes the father couldn't raise the children on his own, and if there were no relatives to take the kids, then they would come here.

You don't get so many in here whose fathers have died, or aren't around. It seems mothers are mostly able to look after their kids, but dads aren't. But my mother couldn't care for me and she thought it would be best for me to go here when I was a baby. I don't miss her as I've never had her to miss.

She does come to see me sometimes, but never more than two or three times a year. Her mother, my gran, comes to see me more; she seems to like me. She brings me sweets and clothes and sometimes takes me out for tea.

Maybe my mother genuinely doesn't like me or maybe she is embarrassed to see me living where I do and not with her. She's never said as much but it's something I think about.

I never knew kids lived with their parents until I was six. I just thought all kids lived like us. I'd never really met kids who weren't from the Homes until I was about eight or nine on a trip to the seaside. The kids on the beach teased us until one of our boys hit one of their boys and they all ran away.

After that, I asked why I was here – I asked my gran, not my mum. Gran told me it was for the best, that my mum wasn't ready to be a mum back then and that she herself was too old to take me.

Then I tried to ask more and she just changed the subject.

3

I come back on the bus from school that afternoon still sick with nerves. Will Glenda be waiting for me, after revenge? She knows – and I know – that I got lucky, and that if she fought me again she would teach me a lesson.

As I get off the bus there's a crowd of kids by the gate. Just girls this time, though. The boys are off playing football; last year everyone was football mad because it was the World Cup, even though Scotland weren't even in it, but this year it's back to being only the boys who are interested. I don't know much about football, but I hear what the boys on the bus talk about and some of it sticks. So if a boy wants to talk to me it means I know something to say back to them.

Jonesy is on the edge of the crowd; she sees me and comes running. I think I'm in trouble and she's going to tell me something bad, but the fight between me and Glenda is old news.

'You've no seen Jane Denton, have you?' says Jonesy.

'Nuh, what's happened?'

'She's done a runner, nobody's seen her. Reckon she's gone off with a fella. She's a good-looking girl. Bet she's shacked up and getting it off some young stud, huh?'

We walk back towards the group of girls. I can see Glenda is in the group and I feel sick again, but we keep walking towards them.

'Who told you?' I ask.

'Rose in her house. Says they are proper jumpin' today in Cottage 12. Says that they've called Jane's family and they've no seen her, but they're going to put polis outside their home in case she turns up.'

As we get to the group, Rose Millar is there answering questions from everyone. The police have been to Cottage 12 and the car is parked near the front steps. They've spoken to all the girls in the cottage about Jane and about where she might have gone and if any of us knew anything.

Glenda is looking at me. I stare straight back at her; she holds my gaze for a second, maybe two, then she nods. *We are not enemies any more*, I think.

After a while Jonesy pulls me away and we walk arm in arm back to Cottage 5.

'She's gettin' a shaftin', that's all it is. She'll be back tomorrow unable to walk, the dirty one. She's going to be so embarrassed when she walks in. But who cares about her? Let's talk about you, you crazy nutter. You're the girl that done Glenda McAdam; ding dong the witch is deid, unreal.'

'Get away.'

'Get away? You're the top dog now, Lesley, I'm gonnae have to be your skivvy. But that's all right, I know I'm safe now. Don't mess with me, or my pal Les is gonnae get yous.'

She pats me on the back several times just as we are getting to Cottage 5. As we come in, Mrs Paterson, our housemother, is there. I like her. I don't know if she likes me. Sometimes she's nice to me, but other times she can be cruel. She has a pretty face. Her hair is always perfectly set every morning before we come down; I never know how she does it. It is jet black and shaped like a crash helmet that men with motorcycles wear. She has a fringe that's level as a ruler and at the back it just touches her collar. She always makes sure us girls have brushed our hair before we leave the cottage each morning. She's said before she doesn't want other houseparents to see the kids from our cottage and think, *They don't have standards in that house.*

She likes to dress smart, too; I suppose she thinks if she looks good it will make us want to look good. Jonesy doesn't really care but I try to do my best.

'Whit's going on, you two?'

'Jane Denton's done a runner, miss,' says Jonesy. 'Gone off with a fella.'

'How do you know this?' says Mrs Paterson.

'Everyone says so.'

'Well, everyone might not be right, you know.'

'Yes, miss.'

Mrs Paterson opens the door to see what's going on outside, before shutting it again.

'Right then, Jonesy, upstairs and git your hands washed, they're a mess.'

I go to go up with her, but Mrs Paterson grabs my arm. 'Not you.'

'Miss?'

She moves me round to look straight into my eyes. 'I will not have young ladies of this house fighting. Do I make myself clear?'

'Yes, miss.'

'And, Lesley ...'

'Yes, miss?'

'Well done, you.' She squeezes my arm. 'You're a brave wee girl, but don't ever do that again, you hear? Now, have you had your tea? I think Cook has left it out for you.'

I smile at her and she smiles back. She does like me. I feel warm all over and safe for the first time today.

*

In the evening all the talk is of Jane Denton. Jonesy is telling everyone just what she thinks she's getting up to while we're all stuck here. I don't know where she's learnt all this stuff, not from me. She can be quite crude when she puts her mind to it.

Everyone's buzzing about it. My fight is forgotten. It was only this morning, but it's old news. I am so tired after not sleeping last night, and not eating breakfast or hardly any dinner. I hope Jonesy doesn't keep me up tonight with her tales.

I know Jane. She used to live in our cottage a few years ago, though she's fifteen or so – three years older than me – so I've not really spoken to her since she left. She's pretty; she's got this scarf and she knows all the boys like her.

I'm not surprised she's got a boyfriend. When she walks down the pathways all the boys watch her. I wonder if she even knows they're doing it – they pretend that they haven't seen her and then as soon as she's gone past they all turn round and nudge each other.

Maybe one day the boys will do that when I walk past. They don't at the moment. I'm not ugly, but I'm not one of the ones they go crazy for. It doesn't matter anyway as none of the boys our age are interested in girls; they're only interested in football and hitting each other, and I can't tell which one of these things they like more.

If people say anything about me when I go past it's something about being stuck up or a swot. I'm not stuck up. I might be a bit of a swot compared to them, but that's only because I like the schoolwork. They just hate me cos they hate all school, they can't understand how anyone can like it. Besides, I don't care what they think, I'm going to leave here one day, and if I can leave with qualifications, it means I have a better chance of never having to see them again.

I lie on my bed and do my homework while Jonesy, Pam, Mary and Shona look out the window. They're watching people going past, and squeaking whenever they see another police car.

Pam thinks Jane Denton will be fine, she's just 'done

a runner', which is a common occurrence in the Homes. Jonesy, of course, thinks she's off with a man. Mary and Shona think she's been kidnapped. I wish they would go downstairs while I'm trying to work. I don't say anything, though, I just let them get on with it.

At lights out they are still talking about it. Mr Paterson comes in specifically to tell them to shut up. I think of saying, 'And so say all of us,' but I don't, I just lie there in the dark thinking how much I love that gate.

4

My first memory is of falling down the steps at the Homes and cutting my arm. I must have been three or four at the time. I was running out of the cottage with some of the others when I stumbled. I put my arm out to break the fall but the speed I was going I missed getting it down on the top step so I went down the two steps and landed on my arm and shoulder.

I was wearing short sleeves so I got badly grazed and blood started to come out. I remember lying there calling for help and crying. Someone came, an adult, though I don't remember who, and they took me to the infirmary over the other side of the Homes.

Jonesy was there then. I remember her trying to hug me as I cried, as if she was trying to squeeze the pain out of me.

Jonesy is Morag Jones. She is my best friend. She has been in my cottage as long as I can remember and always has the bed next to mine. Even when we have to move beds, which we are made to do each year, she will somehow arrange it so that within a few days we are sleeping next to each other again.

They did once try to have us permanently on different sides of the room, but Jonesy just talked non-stop, and she would talk over the other beds to me, until the people in between moved so she could be next to me.

Jonesy has always been a bit scrawny. She eats anything that comes near her, but she's built like a skinny dog, all bones and excited energy.

We are going to be friends for ever and when we leave the Homes we are going to go and live in Glasgow and get a flat and get boyfriends who will buy us nice dresses.

She sometimes gets us into trouble with her never-ending talking, and she gets the odd belt for it. She will cry and be quiet for the day afterwards, but then she will start again. You can't stop her talking. In science we have learnt about an unstoppable force and an immovable object. Jonesy's talking is an unstoppable force.

We are both twelve. She is obsessed with boys and when we will get boobs and how we can make ourselves pretty. She wants to marry a soldier when she is older. She says they get regular money and they are away a lot so she can have the place to herself. Her dream husband isn't such a dream that she wants him around all the time.

I don't know who I want to marry. I certainly don't know what job he will have, but I want him to be kind, and I want him to be smart, and have a nice suit that he will wear to take me out, and I will have a nice dress, and when we walk past people they will think, *She looks nice, I bet they have some money.*

Jonesy and I always look out for each other. The Homes is a dangerous place and you need people to look out for you, your 'team'. The adults aren't always that bothered so unless you have people who can back you up, you are in trouble.

There are a couple of little gangs that the boys are part of. I think that some of them are part of it so the other gangs can't pick them off. The older girls in our cottage look out for us, which I am grateful for, but then they can be nasty sometimes if they are bored and want someone to pick on. It's like they won't allow other people to pick on us, but they will pick on us if they want. Like we are their toys to play with.

Me and Jonesy, for ever joined at the hip. 'The Chatter Twins', Mrs Paterson calls us. We look so different, we act so different, but we are definitely twins who are lost when we are separated for too long.

Having a friend like her makes it bearable to get up in the morning. You need someone like Jonesy in a place like this. She can be a bit annoying sometimes but everything else about her more than makes up for it.

5

The next morning there's a scrambling up the stairs then the door is kicked open.

'She's deid!' comes the cry from Jonesy. 'She's deid!'

'Who's deid?' asks Shona as she jumps off her bed.

The other girls crowd round Jonesy; she's bent over panting. 'Jane ... Denton ... deid ... the woods.'

'Jesus bloody Mary and Joseph,' says Pam.

'Holy shit,' says Shona.

'Oh Jesus,' says Mary.

Eldrey says nothing. She doesn't talk much.

The room is lit up with excitement, we've never heard news so bad. I don't say anything either; I'm stunned. We all thought Jane was going to be with that fella she was supposed to be seeing.

Jonesy recovers her breath a little. 'I saw her body, there was blood everywhere, it was disgusting.'

'Where was it?'

'The woods over the back, behind Cottage 12. I was going to get the post and I heard all this shouting and screaming and some people were running away from it and others were running to it. When I got there everyone was just stood round her staring.'

'Didn't anyone try to save her?' I say.

'They couldn't, she was too deid. It was obvious she was deid, her eyes were bulging out and everything. I've never seen a deid body before, it was horrible.'

'Eurgh,' says Pam.

'Do you want to go and see it?' Jonesy asks.

'No,' says Pam.

'Yes,' say Shona and Mary.

Eldrey still says nothing.

I say, 'I dunno, it's wrong, isn't it?'

Outside we hear sirens.

Everyone looks out the window as police cars and ambulances go up the path. Kids are standing in the porches of their cottages, trying to find out what's going on.

We see Mr Gordon, the Superintendent, storm down the path to a police car. He looks so angry. Someone is going to get it really bad today.

Mr Gordon is a bastard. It's funny that so many of the children here really are bastards, but the Homes are run by another sort of bastard. Jonesy calls him the 'Bastard of the Bastards' but never when adults are around.

If you get on the wrong side of him, you are going to have a very hard time at the Homes. He likes me because I work hard, but I am still so scared of him that sometimes I think I will wee myself if he looks at me badly. I just try to keep out of his way. I've heard the stories of what he's done when he's angry; I don't know if they're true, but I don't want to find out.

He is a bald man who always wears a suit, and he constantly looks like he has been stung by a bee, but is trying not to show you how much pain he is in. It seems like his body is trying to burst out of his clothes. I don't know if he got big after he bought them or if he bought them small so it showed up his size; either way, when he is walking you get out of his way.

'Back in your houses!' he barks. 'Back in your houses or it's the belt!' Other grown-ups are issuing the same orders as they follow in his wake.

We run down the stairs and stand on the porch of Cottage 5. Mr Gordon is talking to a policeman and Jonesy is edging nearer to hear what they are saying. *You're gonnae get killed next if the Super catches you*, I think. And he does catch her. While listening to the policeman talk, he gives Jonesy a stare that could stop a tree falling.

Jonesy comes back to us and we go back into the house. Everyone is listening to her as she has all the information. She has seen the body. She describes it over and over again: the stab marks all over Jane's chest, in her neck and even her cheek.

'Her knickers were off, just sort of on one leg by her ankles,' said Jonesy.

'Why would you take your knickers off unless you were having a wee in the woods or a grown-up told you to? Why would someone stab you for that?' says Eldrey.

'You're an idiot, Eldrey. Someone's done something to her. Raped her,' says Jonesy.

'What's raping?' says Eldrey.

'It's when they stick it in you but you don't want them to.'

Eldrey looks thoughtful. No one asks any more questions.

By the time she has finished, I can see the body every time I close my eyes and all I can think of is Jane. Why would someone do that? How could they do something like that here? The woods are only three hundred yards away; the killer could have walked past our front door.

'Didn't she use to live here?' says Shona.

'Aye,' says Mary. 'Left about six years ago to go to a cottage where she had more friends.'

'You can move to be with your friends?' asks Pam.

'You have to have friends first.' Jonesy gives her a look, then carries on with more of the details. When Jonesy finally stops talking, we don't know what to do next. We are supposed to have breakfast and then go off to school. How can we go on as normal after what has just happened?

Mrs Paterson walks in and says, 'Right, you lot, I want you to have eaten your breakfast and have your school uniform on in the next fifteen minutes or there'll be trouble.'

No one moves until she says, 'Don't make me get Mr Paterson, because then you'll be in real trouble.'

Mr Paterson is not just a threat; he is the punishment. I am not sure what Mrs Paterson sees in him. He's quite grumpy, and for a man who has to work with kids he doesn't seem to like kids very much. Perhaps he thinks that it is Mrs Paterson's job to care about them, and his is just to dish out the punishments.

I wouldn't say he was handsome – Mrs Paterson is definitely the better-looking of the two – but she does like him, even if he is a little shorter than her. She never wears heels as he would look even shorter still. If you mention that he's short, you are for it. And not a one-off, you are going to get it loads. Jonesy did once and she gets it loads off him. That said, there are some girls he just takes against in here. I am usually fine unless I have done something really bad, which I rarely do.

6

Each cottage has children of all different ages, but the same sex, so as to keep us apart. Not that it always works. Some of the older girls in our cottage have come back with the remnants of the woodland floor on their backs, and everyone knows what they have been up to.

The price of ever being caught is that you take such a beating you'll think twice about doing it again.

The Patersons are quite strict houseparents compared to some of the others. When you go to other cottages their houseparents do seem kinder, but then maybe that is because we are guests and they are as strict as Mr and Mrs Paterson once we have gone.

There is also a cook for each cottage. They sometimes change, so we just call ours 'Cook'. Our cook has been with us for many years, but we still call her Cook. We get three meals a day, which is much better than many children in 'normal' families get, so we are told.

Religion is strong in the Homes, which you can tell as the names of the roads in the village are things like

Patience Avenue, Holy Road and Spirit Street. The founder of the Homes is buried along with his wife in the church cemetery. He has a strange presence here. When I was very young I would often confuse the image of him and God, and to me he was like a god in that he was around us at all times, and I often had a feeling he was watching over us. There were many paintings of him in and around the village and there is a picture of him in every cottage. I wonder whether he would have wanted that. He doesn't sound like the sort of man who would appreciate pictures of himself everywhere.

There's also a lie that this is a happy place. It's not. When people come to visit – important people like mayors and politicians and famous people – we all have to pretend that everything is lots of fun and we spend our whole days smiling. All the grown-ups get scared that one of us will misbehave and tell them what it is really like. If important people think it is fun, fun, fun here, they will never do anything to make it better.

There are around twenty-five children living in Cottage 5. I think we have a good cottage. The sort of 'middle' girls live in our room. Then there's a room for the 'big' girls, who we are all a little scared of but look up to at the same time, and a larger room for the younger girls, who we can get to do what we want. Finally there are a couple of babies that we help to look after.

Some other cottages are much less nice – Glenda McAdam's, for one – and some of the boys' ones are pretty rough. Cottage 14 is bad as their housefather, Mr Roberts, really likes to dish it out. You can tell boys from that house as someone has always got a black eye or a limp.

We've got two little two-year-olds. I suppose they're not really babies, but they are in terms of the house. Everyone calls them 'the babies'. Some nights we have to help prepare the tea, sometimes we have to lay the dining-room table, sometimes we have to bathe the babies. Their names are Betsy and Alvin. They are usually quite fun to bathe, but they get really excited and you can end up soaked.

They are jolly, though, all smiles, although Betsy bites if you are not careful and Alvin can scratch, but other than that they are good fun. When we get bored we race them. Alvin wins if he's not distracted. Betsy's probably my favourite, but Jonesy likes her too and we often try to be the ones to bathe her.

Jonesy sometimes points out that there are only two willies in the house, Alvin's and Mr Paterson's. Sometimes Alvin pees in the bath. I think he does it on purpose. He looks so happy when he does it that he can't not be doing it intentionally. Jonesy once held him up and pointed him at me when he did it. She's gross.

The babies sleep down at the far end of the landing. We're lucky to be up our end as we are quite far away from them and they can really greet sometimes. I think they put them near the big girls' room so they know how much hard work little children are and don't get pregnant.

7

After breakfast I leave for the bus. I don't want to go; I want to stay to find out more news about Jane Denton. All day at school I think about nothing else. I don't really have any friends at the grammar so I don't have anyone I can talk to. I think of mentioning it to a teacher, but even though this is a good school, and not full of dafties, if they see you trying to suck up to the teacher they can give you hell for it, so I don't do or say anything.

At dinner I sit on the wall where I usually sit, wondering what is happening back at the Homes. I tend to just sit by myself at dinnertime. No one really bothers me, but then I don't really play with the others much. They all have their own groups that they keep to. I speak to them in class and sometimes when we are eating but mostly I just keep to myself.

Usually I am delighted to be away from the Homes; today I am missing it, everything is going on and I am stuck here desperate to get back.

When the bell goes, I rush to the train station and

make an earlier train than usual. At the bus stop by the station I see one of the older boys who also comes from the Homes. Usually he travels with his friend, Ronnie – I have never seen him alone before, and that makes me brave. I ask him if he knows anything about Jane. It turns out I know a little more than him, so he is interested. I tell him Jane Denton used to live in our house but left when I was about six and she must have been nine. I have never spoken to him before but because of this we have a reason to talk.

His name is Daniel and he is fifteen. I've always thought him and Ronnie are super smart. I try not to bother them, and stay out of their way when we are on the bus, but this is different now; this is an emergency.

We talk on the bus on the way back and when we get off he says, 'Bye'. He's never said 'hi' or 'bye' to me in my life, but it seems normal because of the situation.

I sprint to my cottage and he to his. It has been the most exciting day the Homes has ever seen and I've missed most of it.

I get into the house and I can't see Jonesy. I rush upstairs and she isn't in our bedroom and neither are the other girls. I go down to the kitchen and Cook says they are away over near the church so I turn and run there as fast as I can.

*

When I find them, they are in a huddle by the small group of trees at the bottom of the path that leads up the hill to the church. I am out of breath when I get there.

'What do you know?' I say, panting like crazy.

But they don't seem to know any more than they did this morning, though Jonesy was happy to recite it again, that Jane Denton's body was found in the woods behind Cottage 12. She had been stabbed in the face, in the throat, the legs, the chest. Her hands and fingers were also cut, showing that she had put up a fight to protect herself.

'Whit was she doing in the woods?' I ask.

'I dinnae know?' says Jonesy, as if I have offended her.

'Just askin',' I say. 'Do they know how long she had been deid, like when she was killed?'

'I dinnae know, but the last time anyone saw her was yesterday dinnertime, so it could have been anytime between then and this morning.'

'Well it wouldnae have been this morning, would it?' says Shona. 'No one gets up and stabs someone before breakfast. It would have had to have been last night.'

'Why'd you say that?' says Pam.

'Cos if it was in the afternoon someone would have found her body before, right? If it'd been in the evening or at night, that's why she's been there a bit.'

'So where was she all afternoon, then?'

'I dinnae know, I'm no a psychic,' she says, as if we're blaming her.

I keep thinking of more questions but there is no one to ask. Did Jane know the person who killed her or was it a stranger? I don't know about the others, but I feel scared and at the same time excited.

We don't know where we should go. Should we go back to the cottage, or go to the woods where the body was? They have taken the body away but apparently there are police still up there. Someone said there were journalists at the front gates of the Homes trying to get kids to speak to them.

There are other groups of kids dotted around the grounds: groups of four or five, all doing the same as us and speculating. There are no boys playing football anywhere. The boys always play football until they are told to come in but Jane's death seems to have stopped them.

The minister, Mr Samson, comes out of the church to talk to Mr Sharples, who is pushing a wheelbarrow. We watch them talk for a while, then Mr Sharples leaves. We look up the hill to see what Mr Samson is going to do, whether he is going to invite us into the church to offer some words of wisdom or try to explain it to us, which he usually does if something bad happens. In the end he tells us all to go back to our cottages as standing around gossiping won't help anyone.

This isn't gossiping. Gossiping is talking about if this girl likes that boy. Someone is dead at the Homes. I don't say that, of course. He may be a man of God, but the minister is not averse to someone getting the belt. Not that he does it himself. He tells the Super or your house-father and you get it a day or two later. 'A belting from God,' Jonesy calls it. Once I came home and Jonesy was walking funny. 'Whit's wrong with you?' I said.

'Got a message from God,' she said.

'Oh aye, what's he say?'

'No talking in the pews,' she said, and pulled down her skirt to show me her red raw behind.

8

The following morning all the children in the Homes are called to the Central Hall.

The whole Homes only ever gets together once a year, for Christmas. The Central Hall is the only place big enough for us all to fit at the same time, and even there there's so many of us you can't sit down, so we all have to stand.

We get told this is happening at breakfast, and get led across to Central Hall by Mrs Paterson.

It means me and the others who go to the grammar school will be late.

Me and Jonesy walk hand in hand. 'It's about Jane, it's got to be about Jane,' she says.

'Of course it's about her,' I reply. I squeeze her hand. I feel bad again that this is exciting.

We get in the Central Hall and some of the adults are shouting, 'Wee yins at the front, big yins at the back.'

Me and Jonesy are sort of middle yins, so we pick a spot in the centre. Jonesy spots Kelly McDowell, who comes and joins us with a new girl who looks dead scraggy. Jonesy hangs out with Kelly at school as they are in the same class and she is probably her best school friend, not best house friend or best friend-friend like I am. Kelly's in Cottage 2 and the messy girl is probably from there too. I'm glad she's not in Cottage 5 as she looks like she might have fleas because she keeps scratching.

There's a lot of chat going on. Everyone is talking when Mr Gordon gets up on stage. The Superintendent says nothing, and then, in a second, the room goes quiet. He need do nothing up there. Eight hundred kids and silence, it's amazing. They are as scared of him as I am.

Jonesy squeezes my hand again and I squeeze back.

He doesn't shout, he just talks, but he talks loudly and clearly, so everyone in the hall can hear.

'Right, I am sure you are all aware of what happened yesterday. It is a sad, sad day for everyone here, and I am sure for you, and those who knew Jane closely. Our number-one aim here at the Homes is to keep you safe, to get you a good education and learn the teachings of the Lord. But keeping you safe is first, second and third on our list of things to do.

'This is our responsibility, but we also need your help. We need you to look out for each other, and we need you to tell us, and in particular to tell your houseparents, when you suspect someone may be in trouble.

'With this in mind, I have brought Eadie Schaffer to come and talk to you. Many of you may know her—'

Jonesy gives me another squeeze. 'You know her, you know her!'

'She works as a psychologist to the Homes so if any of you have any problems, she is here for you to talk to should you need it. And she wants to talk to you this morning, so be quiet while I bring her up on stage.'

There's a murmur in the hall. The Super turns to look at everyone and the murmuring stops.

Eadie comes on stage wearing a dark blue jacket and blue skirt with a cream blouse. Her hair is tied back. She's quite young to be so important.

I have to go to see her every once in a while. They like to keep track of me. They never tell me why, but Jonesy says it's because I'm freakishly clever and they have to keep an extra special eye on the freaks. I've never asked why she does it, but it's really nice to talk to her, she's super-super smart.

I go on Saturday mornings, or in the week after I get back from school. My school only does Monday to Friday. The one at the Homes has religious education on Saturday morning, so when everyone goes to that, I go and see Eadie. I can call her Eadie and she doesn't mind; actually, she says she prefers it.

We talk about anything. There's nothing I am not allowed to talk about, which is great as if there's anyone annoying me I can just complain to her for half an hour, or longer if there's no one to follow afterwards. In fact I don't even have to talk. One time I was having trouble with my homework and it was worrying me, and she said to run home and get it and we would go through it together. It was great. She is great.

'Good morning, children. Some of you may know me,

some of you may not. I am the psychologist dedicated to the Homes. My job here is to help you if there is anything bothering you, particularly in relation to your thoughts or feelings. I wanted to talk to you this morning about what happened here yesterday. Now obviously what happened to Jane Denton will have been a terrible shock to you all. It was a cruel and devastating act that is very hard to come to terms with.

'Many of you will be having strange feelings that you may never have had before, feelings of loss and of sadness. This was a tragic event that happened to someone we know and where we live. What I wanted to say to you is that if you need to talk to me, or any of the houseparents, we are here to help you, all you need to do is ask. We are here to listen, and we are here to support you.

'My office is on the second floor of the hospital building, about a hundred yards up from the front entrance for those who have never been. If you want to just turn up you are welcome to do so; you may have to wait, but I *will* see you. Or you can ask your houseparents to make an appointment for you.'

'*She's so nice*,' whispers Jonesy. Others start whispering too, and the murmuring gets increasingly loud.

The Super gets back up on the stage. His face is twitching with menace, he looks at us like we are small insects that he hates, but even though he hates us it's his job to protect us, so that is what he has to do.

This time he doesn't use his powers. 'QUIET!' he calls out.

We go quiet again.

'Now remember what has been said. Keep safe, keep vigilant, and most importantly, keep together. An incident like this is terrible but it is also incredibly rare and whilst I do not wish you to be scared, I do need you to be careful. We will leave the hall two rows at a time. Mr Reynolds will let you out from the back. No pushing – I SAID, NO PUSHING.'

We wait our turn to get let out. It takes about ten minutes until we are all outside.

'So you talk to her every week? She seems amazing,' says Jonesy.

'She is. You should talk to her. You go in there, talk to her and then come out feelin' so much better.'

'Aye, I might,' she says, 'even if it is just to get out of RE.'

'I've told her all about you.'

'She knows about me?'

'Aye, of course she does, you're mah best pal so we often talk about you.'

'What does she say?'

'Nuthin', she just listens.'

'She doesn't tell you what to do?'

'Nuh, we work out what to do together.'

Jonesy and I walk back to Cottage 5. We walk in silence until Jonesy says, 'I can't get the sight of her out of my heid. Every time I close my eyes I see her body covered in blood. I'm scared, Les.'

I squeeze her and tell her it will be all right, but it's not what I think. I'm scared too, and I just want to feel safe. Why would someone kill Jane? I bet she never hurt anyone.

I say goodbye and Jonesy goes off to the school and I walk towards the bus stop to wait for the next bus. The other three grammar school kids come and stand with me. I don't talk to them, but I do listen in to their conversation to see if they know anything that I haven't heard. Ronnie says to Daniel, 'Why did they have to kill a pretty girl? There's plenty of ugly girls round here we wouldn't have missed.'

Amanda Bell, the other girl who gets the bus, tuts. She looks at me as if to say, 'These two are idiots.' I nod in agreement, but we don't say anything – she's fourteen, so I'm usually too scared to talk to her.

When the bus comes, we all get on and sit in our separate areas. Daniel doesn't even look at me. It's like yesterday's conversation never happened.

9

I go to the grammar school in town. I go because I passed my qualifying exam, or qualy as we call it, last year. I was so happy to pass it I could have cried. I studied hard for it and it was worth it. The others in my room took it too but didn't pass. Jonesy didn't expect to pass, but she was still happy for me.

Shona was less happy for me. The school told her she had passed her exam, then a week later they told her they had made a mistake and that she hadn't. She was so angry. She blamed me for it. It wasn't my fault she didn't pass or that they mucked up the marking but that didn't matter to her. They wouldn't let her take the exam again either, they said their decision was final. For months she wouldn't speak to me and she tried to turn the others against me. It was awful.

In the end I was the only one in my year who did pass the exam. I knew what it would mean; I knew I would have to go to a different school, but I knew it would be a better school, for brighter kids, with fewer dafties and people who didn't want to be there.

I never told anyone, but I didn't find the exams that hard. I pretended it was impossible, as did all the others. They wouldn't like it if they knew. If anything, I like exams, I like the questions, figuring them out and getting to the answers is just the best feeling. Like when you think it's impossible, then you look at it again and it all becomes clear.

Sometimes I can't get an answer, and when that happens the question just sticks in my head. Sometimes I will be doing something totally different and the answer will pop in. It's too late by then but it's nice that my brain carries on trying to work it out while I have moved onto something else.

Going to the grammar school means I have to work a lot harder, I have more homework and I have to travel for an hour there and back. I am fine with all these things as I know why I am doing it. I am getting smarter, learning more and I'm enjoying it, though again I would never let anyone know that.

On Sundays we sometimes have religious quizzes at the Homes. Everyone has to work together as a cottage. If you get an answer right, you get a point. If you win you get lots of sweets for the cottage. I study hard for the quizzes too. I get lots of the questions right even though there are much older girls in our cottage. When we win Shona is happy enough to eat the sweets but deep down I think she still doesn't like me.

Because I go to the grammar school, my day is different to the others in my cottage. My school is ten miles away, and when I get up I am the only one who has to put on a school uniform. No one else has to, as they go to the school in the grounds.

My uniform is a white blouse with a tie that is black, red and yellow. I have to wear a grey skirt and a black blazer. It's hard wearing the uniform at the Homes as you stand out and it makes you a target for kids to shout at when you walk past.

I have to get downstairs and have my breakfast quick. My job in the morning is to make the porridge for the house, so I get in the kitchen early with Cook and get that going as soon as I can. I eat mine, then get my bag and head off to the bus stop.

The bus is a Garner's bus, cream on top with the bottom half cherry red. You can see the top cream half above the hedges as it makes its way down to our bus stop. If you miss it you might have to wait another half-hour for the next one so I always make sure I'm early.

We are the last and first stop on the bus route so when we get on there are no other people. They get on later, but when we get on it's just us four Homes kids and the driver. The driver is often the same man who will say hello to us. He doesn't say hello to other passengers, so I wonder if he feels sorry for us because of where we come from. The bus takes us to the railway station and then we get the train to town, and walk on to the school.

School finishes at 3.40 p.m., then it's train and bus back, and I get back to the Homes about 6.15. Everyone in our house eats at 5 p.m. so Cook usually puts some food aside for me. It's a long day but it's worth it and even when it's tough I am still grateful that I get to go there every day instead of the Homes school.

Jonesy can't believe some of the stuff they teach us at the grammar school. The chemistry stuff is amazing; they never teach anything like that at the Homes school. It's fascinating and you come back with your head full of facts and ideas. Maths is my favourite; I absolutely love it. If I had my way I would do maths all day every day. If I have maths homework I do it on the train as I can't wait to get home to do it. There's something so complete about it, when you get it right, you are right, and there's that feeling when you land upon the answer and you just know you've cracked it.

But more than that, there's a moment when you are doing a maths problem and you are so involved in it, and concentrating so hard, that there's nothing else in the world except the problem; no bullies at the Homes, no mum who abandoned you, no girls gossiping or saying things about you, no people judging you because you come from where you come from, just you and the problem and for a wonderful moment nothing else exists.

We are doing quadratic equations at the moment. I love algebra. When you crack the challenge there's a moment of joy that you've got it, you solved it, you beat it, but it's also followed by a moment of sadness that you are back in the real world, but that's all right because there's always another problem to solve.

10

I am in the cottage kitchen after school eating my tea, whilst Jonesy is running through her thoughts out loud.

'Why would someone kill her?' she says.

'Whit?'

'That Jane girl, why would anyone want her deid?'

'I dunno. Any number of reasons.'

'Well what are they? Come on, Les, you're the brain.'

'They hate her. They're jealous of her. They want her deid or need her deid.'

'Why would anyone need her deid?'

'I dunno, I'm just giving you possible reasons, I didn't say it was *the* reason. Mibbie she saw something she shouldn't, or mibbie she knew somethin' they didn't want people knowing about.'

'Like whit, like a spy?'

'I'm just giving examples.'

'What if the person just liked killin' people?'

'Yeah, that could be a reason.'

'Yeah, they just liked killin' people and they wanted to kill some more people, more people like us ...'

'Don't be daft, Jonesy, people don't get killed for fun.'

'What about those Montrose murders?'

The murders happened seven years ago. A man from Lanarkshire called Peter Montrose killed a lot of women, eight, they think. But they caught him and he went to Barlinnie jail, then they hanged him. Jonesy is obsessed with him. She will bring him up at any time.

'They caught him.'

'Aye, but whit if there's someone else like him, someone else going round killing girls.'

'They've no killed *girls*, they've killed *a* girl. They couldae done it for all sorts of reasons, as I've said.'

'They've only killed one girl *so far*. Even that Montrose had to start with one—'

'Jonesy, if you don't shut up I'm going upstairs to read.'

'I'll shut up.'

'Thank you.'

'Makes you think, though, doesn't it?'

'Shut it.'

*

Later in the evening we hang out at the top of the stairs to eavesdrop on the big girls. The rumour is that Jane was pregnant by the man she was seeing and that's why he killed her, so she didn't have his baby.

At this Jonesy and me share a look but don't say a thing.

44

At bedtime that night Jonesy whispers, 'I don't want to go to sleep, Lesley, just in case.'

'Sssshhhh!'

'Aye, you shush me, girl, but you wait.'

'Night, Jonesy.'

'Night, Les.'

Jonesy is often quite scared to go to sleep, usually because of ghost stories. We have this thing in our bedroom where we tell each other ghost stories. They don't scare me, and the reason they don't scare me is because I know they are made up, and the reason I know they are made up is because when I tell my stories I just make them up.

Shona is the other one who is good at telling stories. I enjoy hers, but I know she makes them up too, as I asked her. The other girls get genuinely scared, it's a bit pathetic, but then it is also a bit funny. Jonesy is the worst for it. It's as if the story comes out your mouth and happens straight in her brain, there is no questioning or calling it for what it is, which is a giant made-up fib. I feel sorry for her sometimes, how she takes everything so literally.

*

'Leeeessssss!' A whisper from the next bed.

'Whit?'

'You awake?'

'Naw.'

'Aye, you are.'

'So?'

'Can I come in with you?'

'Naw.'

'Why no?'

'Go to sleep.'

'I can't.'

'You can. Just shut up and it will happen.'

'I did shut up, but my head won't shut up.'

'I'm going to sleep now.'

'I bet you don't.'

'...'

'Les?'

This conversation happens about three times a week, always after the ghost stories, and I stay silent until she goes quiet.

I have got willpower when I try, and tonight I have to really try.

11

Jonesy and I have the beds by the window as we got in the room first and called them. Once we called them, that was that. We also dived on them so they immediately became ours. Shona and Eldrey are on the far side of the room. Mary and Pam are in the middle. It has been the six of us in this room for the last two years.

Shona and Eldrey came from Cottage 11 when the houseparents left and they thought there were too many kids in there for their replacements. At first we didn't like them because we didn't know them, it had just been Pam, Mary, me and Jonesy before that, but after a while we found out they were friendly.

Out of the six of us obviously Jonesy is the chatty one, but Shona can be quite chatty and bossy too. She can be argumentative and she won't back down if she thinks she's right. If Jonesy isn't about, she's the first one to say something.

Her family situation is quite strange. Her sister and her were taken away from their family for their own safety. Apparently, the dad was very, very bad and used to beat them but also used to interfere with them. She never really talks about it, but she has once mentioned it to me. Her sister is two years older, but she didn't come here, she went to another home, which doesn't make sense. There are a lot of siblings in the Homes. I wish I had a sibling in the Homes; it would give me someone special.

Eldrey was Shona's friend from Cottage 11. She is very quiet. Jonesy and me come as a two, and so do Eldrey and Shona. Eldrey seems to follow Shona round wherever she goes. Shona bosses her about all the time. I've asked Eldrey before when we've been alone why she lets Shona talk to her like that, and she says that she doesn't mind and that Shona is a lot nicer when other people aren't around. I just think it's all a bit unfair.

Eldrey is a proper orphan. Her mum died when she was six months old and her dad tried to look after her, but when she was eighteen months he was hit by the hook from a crane at the docks and it killed him stone dead. She was with neighbours when it happened; they cared for her during the day, but that day he never came back to pick her up. Eventually someone came round in the evening to tell them what had happened.

She got some money out of it. All the dockers put in for a fund and it's being held until she is sixteen.

She got brought here at two years old and always thought, like me, that this is how kids grow up. It wasn't until a relative came to check in on her one time that they explained what had happened to her parents.

I don't know what is worse, her situation or mine. At least she had parents who wanted her, but then they were taken away. I had a mother who didn't want me, but then I have a chance to get back with her as she is still here. Eldrey has no hope of that. To make things worse, Mr Paterson doesn't like her and gets angry with her all the time; she's always getting called into his study for a beating. It's unfair as Eldrey doesn't speak enough to make most people angry. It's awful to say but occasionally you can see why Jonesy gets a belt, but Eldrey is so quiet, and after everything she's been through it seems doubly unfair.

Pam and Mary are a bit of a double act too, in fact the whole six of us get along. We say that we are quite lucky that we all get along and are in the same room. Some of the older girls in their rooms don't get on. They're always falling out and having to switch rooms as one girl doesn't like another. Mrs Paterson says we are much easier to look after than they are. She can lose her temper with them really badly when she has to, but she doesn't with us.

Pam is probably the baby of the lot of us. Although Eldrey is quiet, Pam is small, so we sometimes treat her as being younger, even though she's in the same year. She's got a bit of toughness in her; her family was from Calton and it's rough as anything around there. That's not to say that she's trouble or dangerous. I often thought they put us six together as we are not the rough ones, unlike the McAdam kids. They put them all together – the boys in Cottage 13, and the girls in Cottage 8 – and they put us nice ones all together so we wouldn't have to get caught up with them. Only problem is, sometimes it creates a bit of an 'us and them' thing but I suppose that's better than us becoming one of them.

Mary is the tall one, she's a beanpole. That's what they sometimes call her. She's as thin as a rake. Eats everything but stays really thin. It's strange as she has a younger brother in Cottage 21 and he's really short. Jonesy says it was different dads but I don't dare ask.

Mary has never said why she's here. It will be one of the five reasons: her parents are dead, dangerous, on drink, in prison; or she's unwanted/unable to be looked after. None are better or worse than the other.

Mary is quite clever. I think if she worked hard she could go to my school, but the thing is I don't think she wants to work that hard, as she hears the names I get called for going to a different school and I think she'd rather not stand out.

When Jonesy sees me getting called a swot, or stuck up, she is more likely to do something than I am, even though she has said to me that when they call me stuff it makes her feel proud because it means they can see that I'm better than them. I am not better than them, I am just different and like school more, but she seems to see it that way.

That's our room, I'm quite proud of it, we all get along, we are nice and I like them all. I am lucky, I suppose.

12

On Saturday morning I go to see Eadie. I like talking to her. I think the reason I went to her originally was down to the maths tests. We used to get a test on a Friday, either in maths or English. I was good at English but not great, but the maths tests I loved. I used to get 49 out of 50, every time, 49, 49, 49. I would always get one wrong, but then one time I got 50, then again and again. That's when they told me I should go to see Eadie.

Talking to her, you're not being judged, you can say anything to her, anything that is worrying you, any problems you have. I love the hour that I get with her every other week.

She also deals with the epileptic kids. There are two cottages for them, one for those under fifteen and the other for over fifteens. They get teased mercilessly. The house for those over fifteen is called The House that Shakes, the one for under fifteens is The Little House that Shakes. No one knows what causes epilepsy. Some people say it is the devil inside them trying to get out.

I even like the smell of Eadie's room. The hospital area smells of disinfectant all the time and I associate that smell with going to see her, but her room itself doesn't. It seems strange to say, but it smells of books. There are books all over the room, on shelves, stacked on her desk, on a chair. I don't read much other than for homework. I should read more but it's hard to with Jonesy about, talking all the time. It's almost like I'd have to find somewhere to hide to read in peace, and that wouldn't be very kind to her.

Eadie's are all serious books: psychology books, medical books. I asked her how she got into her job and what she was like at school, trying to work out how she found a way to this. She avoids talking about her personal life; when I ask about her mum and dad or if she has a husband or boyfriend she will always say, 'Now, Lesley, we are here to talk about you, not me.' This always leaves me feeling as if I don't really know her, even though after an hour with her I feel like she is the best adult I have ever met, or more accurately that she really knows me and that someone finally understands me.

That office is the one place in the world I feel safe, where I can just be myself. If I am having a bad day, if I can just hold on until I get to see her, everything will be all right.

I hope she feels the same way about me, that she likes me more than the other kids she sees, as I like her more than all the other grown-ups. I might just be another kid to her, but I never feel like that.

'How are you, Lesley?' she asks as she leans forward in her chair.

'I'm scared. Jane Denton got killed. Someone came into the village and stabbed her until she was deid. Why would someone do that?'

'We don't know Lesley. They are clearly a very bad person, but fortunately there are very few people that bad in the world.'

'Well there's one around here and I cannae sleep properly since it happened. I keep havin' bad dreams, like I am in the woods and there is someone trying to kill me and I have to get back to the cottage but I cannae because the floor of the woods is muddy and my feet keep getting stuck.'

'There, there Lesley, that's normal, that's just your brain working through something shocking.'

'I don't like it.'

'Of course you don't, that's natural. Something shocking has happened. I haven't been sleeping well since Jane died either.'

'Will they catch whoever did it?'

'I am sure they will. This is a small village and the police are going to speak to everyone. I am sure it won't take long. Just remember, if you get scared again you always have me here to come and see, all right?'

*

Me and Jonesy sneak out of the cottage before dinner and walk fast round the back of the houses to the woods. It is now two days since Jane was killed.

Up ahead we see the roped-off area. There's a policeman

standing there, hands in pockets. 'Whit are yous two doing?' he says as we walk up to the rope.

'Nothin',' I say, 'just looking at where, y'know ...'

He laughs at us. 'Oh aye, come to stare like all the others?'

'No, we're gonnae find out who did it,' blurts out Jonesy. I am stunned by this news. We didn't agree to this. 'No one is cleverer than Lesley, she'll work out what happened.'

'I'm sure she will,' the policeman says with a smile.

He doesn't let us go any further, but we can see the poor girl's blood still there. There is a lot of it. If she'd been murdered inside, they would have cleared the blood up, but you can't really clear up blood from a forest floor. It has seeped into the pine needles on the ground and looks like the remains of an old brown puddle.

'Aye, she was lying right there,' says Jonesy, pointing to the bloodstains. 'Her body was all laid out like this ... awful pale n'all.' She does an impression, flopping forward like a puppet with its strings cut.

'Do you think she lay there for long?' I ask.

'Alive or deid?'

'Both.'

'Awww, imagine that, lying there and feeling all the blood coming out of you knowing you are going to die. Do you think she screamed?'

'Aye, course she screamed. Wouldn't you scream if someone stabbed you?'

'Aye, but then why did nobody come?'

'They must have covered her mouth? Or mibbie killed

her straight away with the first stab. Who d'you think done it?' I say.

'Some sick bastard, that's who. Why don't they just round up all the sick bastards and say, "Right, which one of yous did it?"'

'It dinnae work like that, Jonesy.'

'It should.'

We walk further round the rope.

'Hey! Careful where you're walking,' says the policeman.

'Awright yerself,' says Jonesy. 'Don't know why he's so chippy,' she mutters to me, 'she's deid, we cannae make it worse.'

'Evidence, Jonesy, there's evidence in there that'll tell you who done it.'

'Righto, I've had enough,' says the policeman. 'You twos, you've done your looky-looky, time to git away or I'll call someone to *take* you away.'

'Yes, sir,' says Jonesy. 'Right away, sir.'

We walk back to our cottage and sneak in the back door so the Patersons don't know that we were out.

'They really must have hurt her,' says Jonesy, as we're going up the stairs. 'See when I cut my finger, that hurts, but see how much it must hurt if someone sticks a knife in you, and again and again. Aww man that's gonnae be brutal.'

'I know. Poor girl must have suffered.'

'And she must have seen who done it cos the knife wounds were all on her front so the person has come towards her.'

'Aye you're right, like if you were running away they would have been in your back, but if they're in your front you knew them and you were fighting them.'

'Fighting them? Like another girl here? Like a square-go but one of them has a knife?'

'Mibbie?'

'Naw, if there's a square-go there's a hundred people here to watch it. First talk of it and everyone would be there.'

'Mibbie she met someone secretly?'

'Aye?'

'Or mibbie a surprise intruder, and she's tried to talk them into no doing it?'

'It's doing my heid in, Les.'

'Mine an' all.'

'Dinnae tell the other girls we were there tonight.'

'Why no?'

'Just dinnae.'

You can tell when Jonesy is thinking. It looks like her face is trying to squeeze her eyes out, they squint off into the distance. She's working through it all, she doesn't know when she's doing it but she can't stop it.

We go up to our bedroom. There's homework I have to do but I can't concentrate. In the end we lie on my bed gazing at the ceiling with Jonesy starting every sentence with the words, 'Hey, what if ...'

13

In the afternoon, Gran comes to the Homes to see me. The sun's out, so we sit on a bench in the gardens, sort of watching the boys playing football. Enough time has passed since Jane was killed for them to think it's acceptable again. Gran says she's heard the news about what happened to Jane. It hasn't been in the newspapers yet, but she'd heard from a friend who knows someone who works here, so she wanted to come and see me.

She says her first worry was that it was me. I tell her not to be so daft, no one wants to kill me. She then warns me that there are bad people in the world and that you need to keep the good people close to you and safe.

She changes the topic and starts asking me about school and how it's going. She asks what my favourite day is. It's Wednesday when I do double maths and we have started to learn French. Everyone seems to hate French, but I like it. I want Jonesy to learn French so we can talk in secret to each other in a language no one knows. They don't do languages at the Homes school, so I have been trying to teach her.

Gran has been to the village tearoom before coming to our cottage and has brought me two small cakes. I eat one right away and stick the other in my pocket for later.

She's starting to look older. She doesn't have a stick but she might need one soon as her walking is slowing and she rests her hand on things to make sure she's stable. She's sixty-two. She's worked all her life on her feet in textile factories in Paisley. She sometimes brings me scarves made out of amazing fabrics. I love them, but I have to keep them hidden in my box as folk will nick them here. The only person I show is Jonesy and we sometimes wear them when no one else is about. I would never wear them outside; people get jealous of anything they think is a bit flash.

We talk more about how I'm doing at the grammar school, but Gran keeps going back to the stuff about Jane. I tell her all about the Central Hall meeting and being late for school. I don't tell Gran that me and Jonesy went up to the woods where it happened.

Gran is good to me, but she doesn't talk about my mum much. When I've tried to ask, she always changes the subject. Occasionally I will ask just to see if things have changed. They haven't. She always just says, 'Your mum says hi,' but I'm sure she hasn't. I'm not sure Mum always knows that Gran comes to visit, or that she comes so often.

She tells me about this film called *Dr No* that has this man from Scotland called Sean Connery in it. She says he used to be a milkman to her friend's aunt away in Edinburgh. In the film he plays a secret agent. I say it's not fair as we never get to go out of the Homes to the cinema. We get films some Sunday afternoons but they are always really old. I like seeing them, escaping for an hour or so, but what I really, really want is to go to a cinema in a town. Gran says if she can take me out one Saturday, she'll take me to the cinema and we'll see a film together. I get super-excited about this.

She says Grandad hasn't been so well. I've never met Grandad. She talks about him a lot but he's never come to see me. I've asked her to bring me a photo of him but she never does. She says he's got a cough that won't go away and it's causing him to stop working. If he's not working, he's not earning, so things are a little tough for them. She wants him to get out of the city and have a break, and says the air of the Highlands would do him the world of good. He says they can't afford it, but she is saying that he can't afford not to.

She lights up a cigarette and blows the smoke out the side of her mouth. I tell her about my chats with Eadie and she says it's nice that there's someone here looking out for me.

She writes down the phone number of her house. She tells me to keep it safe and that if I get scared I am to go to Mrs Paterson and get her to let me call her. I tell her I will keep it in my secret hiding stash, underneath the big chest of drawers. No one knows about it, not even Jonesy.

She tells me to keep safe, then gives me a big hug.

When I hug her I do it too hard and she ends up blowing the smoke into my hair and coughing.

'Sorry, Gran,' I say.

'Don't ever apologise for a hug, my girl,' she says, and then off she walks to the bus stop.

I go back to the cottage to find out if there's any fresh news from Jonesy.

14

Jonesy has always been in my life. Apparently, we used to walk around hand in hand everywhere as toddlers, and while other children our age wouldn't share with each other we would always share, though not with others, we would only share between ourselves. They called us 'the twins' even though she had ginger hair and was much thinner than me. I had blonde hair at the time but it's since gone darker.

There are one or two photos of us from when we were really little but not many. In the two that I've seen we look happy together, and in both we are holding hands, but Jonesy looks as though she was up to something, even back then.

People say I'm the clever one and she's not, but that's not strictly true, we are just different in the things we are clever in. She will see things that I would never notice; she will see socks that don't match on a girl from twenty yards, she'll notice a teacher is not wearing a wedding ring, or alcohol on a grown-up's breath. She's paying attention all the time; her mind doesn't switch off. It isn't always paying attention to what it *should* be aware of as she's too busy watching everything else, but it's never not switched on.

I really like school but it's never suited Jonesy. They used to separate us in the lessons as I would work and she would want to talk to me, then I would give in and talk. 'See her hair?' she would say, pointing at another girl. 'Never washes it, that one.' I would start laughing and then we would both be in trouble. At ten we ended up getting separated as they moved me and a few others up a year and I ended up taking my qualification exam a year early with Shona.

Her family background is a little clearer than mine but no less bad. She has a mum and dad, she must have to be born, but she's never met them. She was taken away from them in the first three months; she has been told they were 'incapable of responsibly looking after her'. She heard that her mum has tried to get her back but that they won't let her. Her mum doesn't know where Jonesy is, so she shouldn't be able to turn up here, but there's always a chance. I think her mum has been locked up before, there was a rumour about that, but in the loony bin rather than prison.

Sometimes Jonesy wonders aloud about her mum, wondering what she does for a job, what she's like, if she talks as much as she does. I've never heard her talk about her dad.

I don't know if it's better to have a family that don't want you, but which you occasionally get to see and a grandmother who likes you, or one that can't have you and never gets to see you. Neither is great. After a while you don't worry about it, you just get on with your life. I've never heard Jonesy really complain about it. I might sometimes complain but Jonesy never does, she just endlessly wonders. She doesn't even complain when she gets a thrashing. Perhaps she should wonder about the thrashings; maybe she should wonder why she gets so many.

Here's a few things to know about Jonesy:

I've never woken before her.

I've never said the last word before we go to sleep.

I've never beat her into the bathroom in the morning.

I've never seen her go a day without smiling.

She is a joy to be with. The first thing she ever does in the morning is come over to my bed to wake me. I usually tell her to get away, then I'll check the time and if I don't have to get up I'll tell her to go back to sleep. Sometimes she wakes at 4 a.m. and is ready to go; when that happens she goes back to bed and stares at the ceiling until it's acceptable for her to get up again. The other girls in our room sometimes complain, but deep down they love her – she's Jonesy. They'd miss her if she wasn't in the room.

In *The House at Pooh Corner*, there's a character called Tigger, and that is who Jonesy is, she's our Tigger, always up and raring to go, nothing gets her down.

We have to worry about her around Christmas. She's always so excited we have to be careful her head doesn't go pop. From December the first she just has this look in her eyes that we are all living in a wonderland and everything will be perfect as Christmas is nearly here.

Anyway, me and Jonesy, we are a team, we are one. Some people say to me, especially some of the teachers back when we were at school together, 'Why do you hang round with her?' They don't know her like I do, and how great she is, and, yes, she can be a bit annoying at times but I wouldn't swap her for the world.

15

Sunday morning and Jonesy and I are in church, and I can't stop thinking about dinner. I saw the joint of beef that Cook was preparing when I loaded the big stove up with coal before church. I had to scrape out the rubble and ash of the previous batch and put in fresh coal, then light it, but it was hard to concentrate after I'd seen the beef.

Cook was rubbing it with lard and throwing salt and pepper over it. Beef is my favourite roast. We get the best gravy with it; it goes over everything. I just want to lick the plate clean.

In church, Jonesy tries so hard to be good, but she just can't manage it. Jonesy is scared of God. It's usually Jonesy who will try to make *me* laugh in the wrong situation, but in church it's the other way round, it just all feels so silly. Sometimes she turns into someone with a broom handle up her bum, and it seems like she is trying really hard to behave and listen and that will be when I decide I want to make *her* laugh.

The minister holds up some bread and says, 'The body of Christ!' I rub my belly and let out a quiet, 'Hhmmm, tasty.' Then the minister holds up a goblet with wine in it and says, 'The blood of Christ!' and I say, 'Hhhmmm.'

Jonesy squeezes her eyes shut as tight as possible to stop herself laughing. Eldrey and Shona look down the pew to see what's going on. Jonesy is twitching, trying to control herself, and I'm holding my face still as an angel who would never dream of making a noise in church.

When we get out of church, Jonesy pushes me, smiling. 'You're a rotter, whit'd you do that for?'

'I'm so hungry, Jonesy, I cannae stop thinking of dinner.'

We get back to the cottage and it smells wonderful. So often I miss eating with everyone in the week, so Sunday dinner is a real treat for me. All twenty-five of us and the Patersons sit at the big table in the kitchen. Cook puts the meat on the table, and there's roast veg and roast potatoes and gravy and you can see the steam coming off it.

It's Mr Paterson's job to carve the meat, and it's like we are a big normal family for one meal of the week, like all the other families around the country sitting down to their Sunday roast. He makes us bow our heads and says grace. I bow my head and close my eyes. Halfway through I open my right eye to see Jonesy with both eyes open, scanning the room. I shut my eye again in case she sees me, makes a face, and then I end up laughing and getting the belt.

Grace ends and Mr Paterson takes out the big carving

knife and the metal thing he sharpens it on. Swish, swish he goes, five or six times. All I can think is, *Get on with it and give us our food*, but he draws it out like he knows we are craving. He then dishes up the meat, Mrs Paterson does the potatoes, Cook does the vegetables, and the plates all get passed down the table, and Cook hands out the jugs of gravy.

When we all have our plates, Mr Paterson gives us a nod and we start to eat. There is no talking as we are busy enjoying the best meal of our week. Even Jonesy shuts up for the five minutes it takes her to eat the meal.

God, I love Sunday dinner.

16

It's the following Saturday and Mum has come to the Homes. I don't know if Gran spoke to her, but she turns up when I am expecting to see Gran instead. I don't know if she has seen the news; we don't get newspapers in the Homes shops, but I see them when I go to school and back. Maybe she is worried about me. It would be nice to think she *does* worry about me; it would be nice to think she thinks of me sometimes.

Mum tends to come once every few months, probably to check that I am still alive. She looks really sad today, but then she often looks sad when she comes. It could be that she's sad all the time, or that seeing me makes her sad. Eadie said once that she may feel embarrassed that she can't bring me up herself, maybe it breaks her heart to see me. Eadie says I should try to show her compassion as Mum probably finds this hard too.

She shouldn't find it hard, she's my mother, she should find it easy. Other people's mums love them. I don't know why Mum doesn't love me.

She tells me she has been let go at her job and that she's taken to cleaning two pubs in the morning, and a doctor's place in the evening. She says she is very tired. She talks about herself pretty much, she doesn't ask much about me, other than to ask what I know about the murder. I tell her that Jonesy and I went to the place where it happened and saw the blood.

I should be grateful that she comes at all and that I've got a mum.

The conversation isn't a good one. I don't know how she is related to Gran, as Gran is so much more fun. Maybe fun skips a generation in our family; hopefully I've got it, but then I wouldn't want my kids not to be fun too.

Eventually she says she has to go and pick up Lynn.

'Who's Lynn?' I ask.

'My daught—'

'Daughter?' I say. 'You've got another daughter?'

She looks down at her feet, then up at me as if she is going to say something, then down again.

'Forget it,' she eventually says.

'No, Mum, I cannae forget it. I've got a sister? Mum, where is she? Where does she live? Does she live here? Is she at another children's home?'

'No.'

'Well, where is she?'

She won't answer. More silence.

'Mum, can I meet her?'

'No.'

'Well, where is she?'

69

'At home.'

'Whose home?'

'My home.'

'Your home? But—'

She mumbles something.

'But why does she live at your home wit you? Why cannae I live at home wit you?'

'Because ...'

'Because what, Mum?'

'Just be quiet.'

We sit in silence. I look down. I am breathing hard through my nose. I don't want to break the silence, but I just can't understand ...

'Ah hate you, Mum, Ah hate you! I wish I could have had any other mum in the world as they would have been better than you!' I shout as I run back to my house.

And as I am running, I decide for certain that I am never going to speak to that woman again.

17

When I get back to the house I go straight to my bed, hide under the sheets and start crying.

The problem living where we do is that there are six of us in the room, so you are never alone and you can never cry in peace. Eldrey is lying on her front on her bed looking sore, probably thanks to another belting from Mr Paterson, but she kindly goes to get Jonesy, who comes up to see me. Mrs Paterson also comes up after a while.

I can't tell them for a long time, I just cry and cry, and then when I try to tell them what happened I start to cry again.

Eventually I tell them what Mum accidentally said. How the reason she probably never came was that she was at home with her other daughter, the one she chose to keep.

'At least you have a mum,' Jonesy says. It doesn't help.

Mrs Paterson just rubs my back while I cry. I've got snot all over the bed and in my hair so she goes to get a towel and rubs my face clean. She tells me it will be all right.

Mrs Paterson has to be strict because there are so many of us, but sometimes she will sit and listen to you and hold your hand. I say some horrible things about my mum and she lets me. I've often wondered why Mr and Mrs Paterson don't have children of their own. Maybe they can't, or maybe they think they can help more children by working here. It has to have been her idea if that's the case.

The anger passes and I start to breathe normally again. I take out a hankie and blow my nose. Every day I understand a little bit more about myself and why I am here. They should just change the name of this place from 'the Homes' to 'the Unwanted', cos that's what we are, unwanted by our families and unwanted by God.

I ask Mrs Paterson, 'If God didnae want us, why did he have us, or why did we get born to people who didn't want us?'

Mrs Paterson says, 'God wants us all, Lesley. He wants and loves us. Sometimes the path he chooses for us is obscure, but it all becomes clear in the end.'

'But what if that's too late, miss? What about Jane? What if she didn't find out her path before she died?'

'I don't know, Lesley, I can't answer for God. Would you like to speak to the minister?'

'I want to speak to Eadie.'

'I'll see what I can do,' Mrs Paterson says.

I look at her, and I think I have started to see a pattern. Mrs Paterson doesn't mention God much, it's Mr Paterson who says grace, and neither of them goes to church on the weekend, but the moment I ask a difficult question it's 'God loves us all' and 'God has his plan', like it's a giant excuse for the unexplainable.

*

I don't go down for tea. Jonesy doesn't go down either, she just stays with me and we lie together in my bed. I sometimes feel the only person I've got in this world is Jonesy. She tells me I am the only person she has really loved, other than Tim Fitzgerald who's two years older than her, brilliant at football and 'a pure dream', but that if she has to choose between the two of us she will choose me. That makes me smile for a while. Then I am sad again.

I just want my mum to explain why she didn't want me. I will ask Gran when she comes again, but I think she might be in on it too. She must know I have a sister, but then why didn't she tell me? Why are these people lying to me? Do all grown-ups lie?

Today I have gained a sister and lost a mother and probably a grandmother all in one day. Nothing has changed, but what I know now I can't un-know, and it makes me so sick. It's just so unfair.

By the time I fall asleep my head hurts with all the crying. I decide that I am never going to cry again over my mum, she isn't worth it. My tears will only be for people I love and she will never be in that category. I will never expect anything from her so she can never let me down.

18

Sunday morning and after church Jonesy suggests we go for a walk out the grounds to some fields she knows. I know she is only doing it to try to get me to not think about my mum. I appreciate it but my mind keeps drifting off to thoughts about who my sister is, what she looks like and why *she* gets to live with Mum. In church I hardly sang anything.

We walk up Faith Avenue towards the Homes entrance and there are three men by the road. They come towards us, so Jonesy and I turn right instead of the way we were going. One of them gestures to me and waves as I try to walk off.

'No, hen, no, wait.' He pulls out a notepad and a card of some kind. 'I'm a reporter with the *Glasgow Herald*. I just want to talk to you.'

'To me?' says Jonesy. 'Why do you want to talk to me?'

Quick as a swallow he changes direction and is talking to her instead.

'Well you see it's very important we find out all the

information we can about the murder as it is big news.'

'It is, isn't it? We saw the body. Well, me and some other people – no Lesley here, Lesley didnae see the body, but she did come up the woods with me a couple of days after to see where the body was and there was a policeman, but there's probably clues where she was found, and—'

'Jonesy, shut it,' I say, as quietly as I can so she can hear it and he can't.

'And what is your name, hen?' asks one of the other men. They are all listening to Jonesy, which is making her happy, but I don't like the way they are writing down everything she says.

'It's Morag Jones, people call me Jonesy, but Morag Jones is my full name. Don't have a middle name, posh kids get middle names, I didnae get one, I might give myself one when I'm allowed to do that. How old do you have to be to do that? Sixteen, I would think – I'm twelve now and I live in number five. This is Lesley, she lives in five with me.'

'And what is "five"?' he asks.

'Cottage 5, it's a girls' cottage. They all have numbers. Ours is five.'

'HEY YOU!' comes a roaring voice behind us. It's the Superintendent.

'I THOUGHT I TOLD YOU TO GET TO—'

'Yes Mr Gordon, you told us to get off the grounds and that is what we did.' The reporter sounds scared. It's good to know that Mr Gordon can scare adults as much as he scares us. 'We are not on the grounds. We are outside.'

'Girls, get inside now.'

We walk as fast as we can back through the main gates without it becoming a run. We can hear the Super growling at the journalists behind us, but we daren't turn back to look.

I realise as we walk back that it's taken my mind off my mum, but also it made me realise that the murder isn't just big news at the Homes. It is big news everywhere.

*

Mrs Paterson got word to Eadie Schaffer that she needed to see me. Mrs Paterson's sometimes good like that. It's hard for her, it must be even harder for her husband, in a house with nearly thirty girls, all screeching around all the time. I think that's why he gets angry sometimes and tells everyone to shut up, but it's to be expected. If Mrs Paterson was in a house with all boys I think it would drive *her* crazy. She's said that before to explain when he does get angry. He blows his top and it's scary as anything. I would say he has favourites and girls he doesn't like, but that wouldn't be true. There's definitely ones he doesn't like and has got it in for, and the rest of us he just tolerates.

The key with Mr Paterson is to work out what annoys him – that's where Jonesy goes wrong. She has no sense of what she does that annoys him, and then she gets the belt. If you are too noisy around him, instant belt, but also if you are too meek and mild like Eldrey he doesn't seem to like that either. He also hates running in the house, but all grown-ups seem to hate that.

On Monday morning Mrs Paterson tells me that when I come back from school I should go and see Miss Schaffer and she will stay late to talk to me. At dinnertime I just read a book on my own to eat up time and distract myself. It's a good book, called *Kidnapped* by Robert Stevenson, so I think about the character Davie's troubles instead of mine.

*

When the bus home drops us off, I walk back towards Cottage 5 before realising that I should be going to the hospital building to see Eadie. She's with some other kid, so I wait outside her room. If you go to the doctor you wait your turn but you are never in there more than five minutes; with Eadie, a person can be five minutes or they can be an hour, you never know. She never rushes you and she always listens completely until you are done.

This time, I have to wait half an hour and spend the time reading my book. It means my tea will be cold, but if I am her last visitor of the day I don't have to worry about others waiting for me to leave.

It's worth it.

The smile she gives me when I come in feels so nice that I nearly start crying straight away but I don't. She must have had a good chat with Mrs Paterson, because she knows everything that has happened.

She lets me talk and talk about how unfair it is, and what a terrible person my mum is. She doesn't tell me I mustn't say that, she just lets me talk and talk. It is gone half seven by the time we are done.

When we are finished I feel so much better. I could have said nothing – just being in the room with Eadie makes me feel better – but getting it all out is a relief.

*

Back at the cottage, a bowl of thick vegetable soup and some bread have been left out for me. Cook has put it aside in the kitchen and covered it with a plate. The bread is hard and the soup is cold, with a skin on it that I use a spoon to scoop off, but it tastes good, and I drink some milk with it.

Jonesy comes down and finds me in the kitchen eating. I tell her that Eadie is so great, that she's the only adult who's ever nice to me all the time.

Jonesy says no adult has been nice to her all the time. She says she likes the ones who just don't belt her too often and that is good enough for her. We agree that kids are nicer than adults and hope that we don't become horrible people when we get older.

We talk all evening. It's getting to be summer and it's lighter for longer. When it's time to go to bed it's still light outside. We pretend to sleep for a while, then Jonesy joins me in my bed.

19

'Les?'

'Whit?'

'Leeesss?'

'Whit?'

'Leessssssssss!'

'Whit is it!?'

Jonesy is jerking her head as if her ear has been caught with a hook and is being yanked by a fisherman.

Shona and Eldrey are with us in the kitchen, and I am eating my tea after school. They turn to look at Jonesy to try to work out what she's doing. It's not hard, she wants to talk to me and she wants them not to be there, but I am tired and hungry and whatever it is can wait.

Except it can't. Jonesy is clearly going to burst if she's not able to tell me something. She's staring at me from behind the other girls, eyes popping out of her face. Shona is in the middle of a story about a boy who spoke to her today. Me and Jonesy don't care. Eldrey will listen to anything to keep the peace, and Shona will keep

79

talking until she's told to shut up, or there's no one there to listen to her.

There's this cruel thing the girls in the cottage sometimes do; I say the girls, but it's Jonesy, mainly. It's like a choo-choo train, and it starts off slowly, as if the train is far away. It goes, 'Dinnae-care, dinnae-care, dinnae dinnae care,' and then it gets louder: 'Dinnae-care, dinnae-care, dinnae dinnae care,' until eventually it becomes, 'DINNAE-CARE, DINNAE-CARE, DINNAE DINNAE CARE!' and everyone is joining in and whatever you were talking about you can't carry on with it any longer. It's cruel and unfair and Jonesy starts doing it now.

Shona knows what it is and knows what's coming so she stops her sentence, declares, 'You lot can all get stuffed,' and storms out of the kitchen. Eldrey looks at us two as if she doesn't know whether to stay or go with Shona; if she stays, she'll be lumped in with us. Jonesy solves the problem by twitching her head to imply Eldrey should get away, and she does.

So now we're left alone. I'm just finishing the last of my carrots and tatties.

'God, I thought they'd never go,' she says.

'Really?' I say with a look.

'I've got to tell you something, something big.'

'Aye.'

'No it's big, I mean big, big.'

'Aye.'

'Les, I think I might have done something bad, but it might be good. I found something, and you have to

80

promise not to tell anyone what I found. And I mean *promise*, promise.'

'Jonesy, come on, just spit it out.'

'Promise?'

'Jonesy,' I say in my stern voice.

'All right, all right, but this is ... oh this is ... Right. You know Jane, deid Jane, stabbed Jane, stabbed deid Jane ... I found her diary.'

'Whit?'

'I did, when you were at school. Nobody knows I've got it. I found it – well, retrieved it.'

She's right, this is big; this is enormous. Ordinarily I would say, 'You're lying,' but I know Jonesy better than anyone and I know when she's lying, and the pure excitement in her eyes means there's only one answer.

'Where did you find it?'

'Well, you know how I'm friends with Brenda who's in Jane's cottage? She took me to Jane's room to show me it, like where she slept and everything. The polis have all been in there and been through everything, her box and all. But like, where do you keep stuff that is top-top secret that you don't want anyone to find ever?'

'In my box and locked.'

'No, the secret stuff, the stuff you don't want anyone to find.'

'I don't know what you're talking about.'

'Les, quit messing, I know where you keep your stash. You hide it under the chest of drawers and wedged in the corner.'

'How did you know about that?'

'I'm no as daft as you lot think I am. So I thought, if that's where Les hides things, I wonder if Jane does the same? So when Brenda goes out the room I lie on the floor and reach underneath just to see if anything's there, and it's like the pools coupons times a hundred – jackpot! She's only got this tiny wee diary. Small, like the size of your hand.'

'Well, where is it?'

'I put it with your stash. When the girls are out the room we can go get it. I need your help, though; it disnae make sense, all weird letters and stuff.'

*

'Beat it.'

'*I want to use the lavvy*,' comes the shout from the other side of the door.

'I said beat it.'

They leave, but then there's a louder banging on the door from Mrs Paterson. 'Whit's going on in there?'

'Just doing our teeth, miss,' says Jonesy. We were smart in that we'd brought our toothbrushes into the bathroom so we would have an excuse if anyone caught us.

'Well get out now, you've been in there long enough,' she says.

There's not a lot we can do but come out, first making sure our toothbrushes are wet in case she checks. We go back to our room.

'Whit were you two doing?' Shona asks.

'None of your business,' says Jonesy.

We're not going to get a chance to look at the diary tonight as the lights go out soon and we've not got torches. Jonesy hops straight into my bed and whispers, 'Whit we gonnae do?'

'Wait till tomorrow.'

'I cannae wait that long.'

'You're gonnae have to.'

'But Les—'

'Shut it.'

'Les—'

'Shut!'

That night is one of the longest in my life. Night of a thousand twitches. Like sleeping next to a puppy with the hiccups.

20

Jonesy is waiting for me when I get off the bus in the evening. She tells me that she tried to read the diary on her own at dinnertime.

'Les, I still couldn't make any sense of it. It's full of initials.'

'You've read it all?'

'The lot. I don't understand it. Are you going to get your tea?'

'Naw, let's go somewhere and read it.'

We scurry to the nearest bench, me carrying my schoolbag and her carrying the diary inside her top so no one can see. We sit down and she shows me. The pages are very small and the writing is cramped. It's in pencil and you can see bits have been rubbed out. But the paper is thin and sometimes the writing has gone through it. Not every day is written on; it seems to be a mixture of the mundane and exciting.

15 March

Met T aft schl by gym. Said I diff frm oth grls. Kssd, nrly sn.

19 March

Grls tkng abt me. Thy nd 2 kp mth sht

22 March

T ddnt lk at me at all tdy, think smth wrng

25 March

T kssd me gnst wll.

'What do you think it means, Les?'

'Well, the first one looks like it says, "Met T after school by the gym. He said I was different from the other girls. We kissed, nearly seen."'

'God, I know that, Les, that's obvious, I'm no an eejit. What I meant was, who is T?'

'I don't know.'

'Well how do we find out?'

I read some more. Lots of mentions of T. Jane seemed to like T more and more. But after the 8th of May there's nothing. The last entry says '*mtg T tmrw, gttg thgs strt*' and that's it, her life over. It's hard seeing her life no longer on paper.

A life that stopped when she had so many empty pages to be filled. I feel a sadness for Jane Denton that I didn't the day she died. Then, it was just shock; I didn't know her well so I didn't feel sad, just scared. Now, seeing the life she had taken away, I feel the loss.

Jonesy and I try to guess who T might be, who we know with that initial. Maybe it stands for something else. Maybe it's a code?

I tell Jonesy this but then say that I don't think Jane was the sort of girl who would have used a cipher. I have to explain what a cipher is. Once Jonesy gets her head round it, she agrees that it doesn't sound like Jane.

My mind is racing. We go back to the cottage and spend the rest of the evening trying out our theories on one another.

'So who is T?' says Jonesy for the tenth time.

'Dunno, but it's got to be one of the boys or men at the Homes. She definitely likes T but mibbie T forces her to do somethin' and she fights back and T kills her. Or what if T sees her with another boy and kills her? Or, or she doesnae like T any more and splits with him and *then* he kills her?'

'It's got to be one of them. Jealous as hell, I reckon, jealous and he's gone, like, "If I can't have you no one can," and he's killed her cos he cannae handle her with anyone else. But who is it?'

'Well they're gonnae be older than her, right? She's no going to be going with a boy younger than her, is she?'

'Who's her housefather?'

'Mr Calder? The fella's a cripple, he's got arthritis up to his eyeballs. Has to use a stick. *I* could take him.'

'Les, if you can take Glenda McAdam, you can take

anyone. Could be you, Les? Did you go in one of your rages? Has your new power gone to your heid?'

'Get off, will you? This is serious. Who do we know whose name starts with a T? Tim Fitzgerald?'

'My Tim?' She snorts. 'Naw, no my Tim, he's too nice, wouldnae be him. Besides, he's fourteen and Jane was fifteen, there's no way she'd be going with him, girls that good-looking don't go with boys younger than them.'

'Tommy McAdam, Glenda's brother? He's her age.'

'Aye, he's a wild one, proper daftie.'

'Right, so Tommy McAdam. There's got to be more Ts.'

'We talkin' first names or surnames?'

'I dunno.'

'Cos probably dozens of kids in the village have got Ts for surnames.'

'Ah, Jonesy, I dunno.'

This goes on for another hour and by the end we have a list of twelve boys of the right age with first names that start with T and fourteen with surnames that start with T. But no one who we think Jane Denton would have wanted to kiss.

21

'Your dog's here,' says Amanda as we get off the bus together.

'Hey?'

'Your dog – your wee pal. She waits for you by the gate wagging her tail. I've seen her do it before.' She's nodding towards Jonesy, waiting at the front gate again, and shouts, 'You wait for her like a wee doggy waiting for its master, don't you?'

'Shut it, curly.'

'Dinnae tell me to shut it, little thing, I'll batter ye.'

'You will not.'

'Jonesy, stop it,' I say.

'Aye, good dog, sit,' says Amanda, staring at Jonesy as she walks off to her cottage.

'Whit you doing talking to her?'

'She's nice.'

'She's a spod.'

'She's no.'

'Aye she is, but it disnae matter, more important things,

Lesley, more important things. I have a question for you. It's a simple question. Are you ready for your question?'

'Aye ...'

'Lesley, am I or am I not a genius?'

'I suspect the answer might be that you are, in fact, a genius.'

'Correct, well done. Now, for an extra point, would you like to know why I am a genius?'

'Yes, Morag Jones, I would very much like to know why you are a genius.'

She's started skipping with excitement. 'What lesson did I have today?'

'No idea.'

'Geography, I had geography. And who did I have it with?'

'Everyone else in your class?'

'Incorrect. Well, correct, but that's not the right answer.'

'So ...'

'Mr Taylor. Better known as the Gorgeous Mr Taylor.'

'And ... are you in love again?'

'Again? I was never not in love with him but I wasnae the only one – and I know something you don't.'

I don't answer or prod her. I wait for her to do it herself.

'Wanna know?'

'Of course I wanna know. Just get on with telling me.'

'T. T in Jane's diary. She's only been going with the teacher!'

'Naw.'

'Aye.'

'Naaaw.'

'Ayyyyyye, I'm telling you. It's got to be T that Jane would be kissing round the back of the school.'

'But it could be anyone.'

'It could, but it isnae. C'mon Les, we went through every boy with the initial T and couldn't think of any that Jane Denton would kiss. Him – she would definitely kiss.'

'Aawwww Jesus, Jonesy, what if you're right?'

'I am right and I've been waiting all day to tell you.'

We've just about got to the cottage by this time, and I stop her. 'Whit do we do now?'

'I don't know. We could tell him we know it's him?'

'No ... no, we tell the polis.'

'How? How do we do that?'

We go inside. Cook has left out a piece and ham for me. I eat it while Jonesy continues to yabber. I don't listen as I am concentrating on my thoughts.

When she's done with her talking and I'm done with my eating I tell her, 'There's four people we can tell: the polis, Mr Gordon the Superintendent, and Mr and Mrs Paterson.'

'I'm no telling the Super, and we don't know anyone at the polis to tell. Let's go for the Patersons. But how do we tell them about the diary, that I took it?'

'Christ, I didnae think about that. Forget the Patersons. What about telling the polis anonymously?'

'Whit's anonymously?'

'When you send something but you don't tell them who you are.'

'Like a letter without writing your name?'

'Exactly. Let's write a letter and send it to the polis to tell them that Mr Taylor was going with Jane and he probably killed her.'

'He couldn't have done it, though.'

'Why not?'

'He's too beautiful. Nobody that beautiful could do a thing like that.'

'He is beautiful, isn't he? Doesn't mean he didnae do it.'

'It disnae seem fair. They'll have to send a beautiful man to prison. Why couldn't it be an ugly man? That way you get rid of a killer and an ugly person at the same time.'

'You're terrible, Jonesy. I hope you never become a judge.'

'Yes you do, you'll want friends like me in high places one day.'

22

'She's here again,' says Amanda as we get off the school bus.

Jonesy ignores her, comes rushing up and grabs my arm and walks me, firm and fast, into the Homes.

'They came, Les, the polis came and they took Mr Taylor away. They came this afternoon. Everyone saw it, EVERYONE. We saw them take him in the car and drive him away.'

'Christ, Jonesy. Did we do the right thing?'

'Of course we did. He was going with her, she probably wanted to end it or tell someone which means he's in trouble, so he's killed her.'

'But did he? All we know is he was going with her. Doesn't mean he killed her.'

'That's for the polis. We just poked them in the right direction with your letter.'

'My letter? It was *our* letter. We both decided to do it.'

'Aye, of course, I just meant you wrote it and posted it. That's got to be why, yeah?'

'Aye, definitely. Why else would they have been here?'

'They could have worked it out for themselves.'

'Nah, they didnae have the diary.'

'What did he look like when they took him away?'

'Like he was gonnae cry. He wouldn't look at anyone, just stared at the ground. He didnae seem like him, like he wisnae gorgeous like usual.'

'Jonesy, it's hard to be gorgeous when they're putting you in a polis car.'

'Aye, but you know what I mean; it looked like him but it didnae.'

'You haven't told anyone about the diary and the letter have ye?'

'No, no, no, cross my heart and hope to die. I widnae do that. You can trust me.'

'I know I can, Jonesy, I just know you get excited sometimes.'

'Nah, I've got this, hen. You and me, putting bad and beautiful men in jail.'

I laughed at this.

'We should write a book, Les – *The Bad and the Beautiful*, about this gang of men who are like unbelievably beautiful, but they are also secret killers and they go around the world seducing women and killing their husbands.'

'You're nuts, Jonesy.'

'I'm a genius, Les, people just don't know it yet.'

23

Another girl has gone missing.

It's been more than two weeks since Jane Denton was killed and now Sally Ward has disappeared. She's not been seen since after school on Friday. That's twenty-four hours and the adults are going crazy. Some of the kids are saying that she was a friend of Jane's, though some say that's not true, and no one really knows what to think.

Earlier today I saw the Superintendent marching across the grounds. Mr Gordon always looks angry, but this time he looked like he was going to kill someone himself.

Mr Paterson is suddenly being protective of us for a change. Just before we sit down to eat, he sticks out his chin and says no one is allowed out of the house after tea, even if we have finished our chores, and that there is going to be a curfew from now on. Other than going to school and back, if we leave the house we must get permission from him or Mrs Paterson.

Sally Ward is fourteen or fifteen, just like Jane Denton was. I don't think there are any rumours of boys. I have never heard of her; she's not one of the ones we know. She's not from a cottage near ours – I think she's in 29 over the other side of the village – and she's probably not pretty. You tend to know who the pretty ones are, and you tend to know the people in the cottages around yours as we are in and out of each other's.

Everyone is so excited at tea. I'm not sure I mean excited, maybe agitated, even more so than when Jane went missing. We are all talking at the same time and the noise is really loud. After saying those things about us being safe Mr Paterson gets angry and starts shouting over us to make himself heard. He tells us we all have to eat in silence and anyone who speaks will be sent to bed without any food.

So we are silent. Jonesy can't bear that; she keeps pulling a face at me. Mr Paterson sees her and makes her stand outside and wait until everyone has finished their tea before she is allowed back in to eat on her own. She hadn't spoken so he couldn't send her to her room.

Jonesy doesn't care, which is her problem. She never cares when she's told off. I don't know how she does it. I hate it when they shout at me.

When we get back to our bedroom all the girls are round Jonesy's bed as she tells them that if Sally is dead too, then that means there's a mass murderer on the loose killing girls at the Homes and we could be next.

'It's like you said, Jonesy, it's like the Montrose murderer, isn't it?' I say.

'Exactly,' said Jonesy. 'He's out killing and raping again.'

'What, you think he's escaped?' says Mary.

'No, I told you, he cannae have escaped cos they hanged him in Barlinnie,' I say.

'What if they hanged the wrong fella?' says Jonesy.

'Naw, they hanged the right fella. No more murders once he was hanged.'

'Aye, until now, that is. Mibbie it was someone else and they've just been lying low. And why do they always want to kill young girls? Can't they kill old men or something, or is it more fun for them to kill kids like us?'

'Whit's going on?' says Mrs Paterson, entering the room.

'Why do they always wanna kill young girls?' Jonesy asks her.

'What on earth are yous talking about?'

'There's a killer on the loose and they are killing young girls.'

Mrs Paterson rubs her face, then fixes Jonesy with a look. 'One unfortunate girl was killed, that's true. But today's event is different. A girl has gone missing – it's happened before; it will happen again. Sally will turn up and you'll see what nonsense you're talking. Now, lights out and go to bed. And if there's any more chat there'll be no film tomorrow.'

A collective cry of 'MIIIISSSSS!' goes up at the threat.

She turns the light out and I know Jonesy is going to say something. I know it.

But she doesn't, she doesn't say anything. For a whole two minutes, and then she says, 'Well, she would say that, wouldn't she? She's just jealous that they dinnae want to kill and rape her because she's too old.'

I lie there shaking my head in the dark.

24

The police have brought sniffer dogs in. They did it while we were all at school so they thought we wouldn't notice, but there are always kids about, and kids always notice.

Dogs' noses are supposed to be a thousand times more powerful than human noses, so they can find where you've been by the smell. The dog handlers got some of Sally Ward's clothes, rubbed them in the dogs' faces and let them try to find her. The dogs went crazy apparently. Ran everywhere but found nothing.

Mrs Paterson watched it from the front of the cottage. She was the one telling us not to gossip, and now she is the one telling us what happened.

*

At breakfast the next day, Mrs Paterson taps her glass with a knife and everyone goes quiet.

'I want everyone's attention, please. Quiet, quiet. I

need to talk to you young ladies and I need you to pay close attention.

'You're aware that there was a tragedy with Jane Denton, and it was very, very shocking and very, very sad. Now Sally Ward has gone missing, which is again very sad. We don't know whit's happened to her, and speculation doesn't really help the situation, but the polis are worried so we should be worried.

'What I am saying is delicate. I don't want you to be scared, but I do want you to be careful; I want you to be extra careful. As you know, you are to come home straight after school, and from now on I would like you to travel everywhere in pairs.'

'Is Sally deid?' asks Jonesy.

'Morag, what did I just say about speculating? It doesnae help. The polis are worried that she is, aye. We just don't know. But I do know this: life is in many ways harder for us ladies. Sometimes people – men – target young women. This could happen to you at some point, and you need to be careful. Keep your wits about you, keep an eye out for each other. Life isnae fair for a young woman, and you need to be aware of that. Don't be naive, don't be complacent. Be alert and have each other's backs; there is a thing called the sisterhood that we all belong to.'

I look around to see if Mr Paterson is there as I am worried that Jonesy will point out that he isn't part of the sisterhood. He isn't there; maybe Mrs Paterson asked him not to be so she could say this.

'I'm just sayin', be careful out there. Out there,' she says, pointing at the door, 'and in the world.'

A tear rolls down her nose.

'Now, let's pray. Heavenly Father, thank you for the food you put before us, and thank you for our health. Please look over us and protect us and keep us in your heart, as you are in ours. Amen.'

'Amen,' we all say.

'Let's eat.'

And we do, in silence. I don't want to break it by talking, and it seems like neither does anyone else.

25

After breakfast I go get my bus. We don't have to be in till ten thirty today as they are showing around the new students for August's intake. Perhaps they don't want us students about to scare them too much. I was so scared when I first went to the grammar school, but I needn't have been; the pupils are much less dangerous than the kids in the Homes.

On the bus, we all discuss what we know about what's happened. I usually sit near Amanda but not near enough to talk. As there are only four of us, we get a double seat each.

Daniel and Ronnie tend to sit at the back and Amanda tends to sit in the middle, although sometimes with them. I did sit at the front on my own but have recently started moving backwards nearer to them. This time all four of us sit near each other in the middle; after Jane's death and the news about Sally it has meant a break in the established social rules.

It's strange that normally we don't usually travel

together as a group. We all go from the same place to the same place, at the same time, on the same buses and trains, yet I wouldn't say we travelled together. Today we do.

Ronnie, who is tall and skinny and has a lot of spots on his face, says that he's heard it was a minister who took Sally because she was impure, as a warning to all other girls. Daniel says he thinks it might have been a werewolf. He is just trying to scare us; he's too smart to believe in werewolves. Amanda says that she has spoken to Sally before – she knows a girl in her cottage a bit. She's been over to Cottage 29 since Sally disappeared and the atmosphere in there is Baltic – all the girls were all crying and are convinced she's dead. They think she had a boyfriend as she had been sneaking out in the weeks before, but no one knew who it was.

None of us really know Sally. We all think she must have been killed, too, like Jane was.

At the grammar school we are the centre of attention; now Sally's gone missing, the newspapers have gone crazy again and all the children want to know what's going on at the Homes. Sometimes they tease us about having no parents and living in the Homes, and are snooty about us, but today we are the most important people at the school. Had I seen anyone suspicious hanging around? Who do I think did it? Are there many policemen about searching for Sally?

Even a teacher asks me what's happening. I tell her what I know, but not that Jonesy saw Jane's body when she had been killed, nor that we went to look in the woods where she was found. As for Sally, I just say that people run away sometimes, but obviously they think she's been murdered too. I feel bad guessing about what's happened but that is all everyone's doing, we know so little – especially why it's happened.

By the end of the school day I am so tired of talking and saying the same things. On the train and bus none of us says anything, we all just stare out of the windows at the fields as they go past.

26

Gran is waiting for me when I get off the bus. Usually you are only supposed to have visitors at weekends, so she must have got special permission, or she didn't ask and just turned up.

I had managed to forget Mum for a bit.

The tearoom is shut so we go and have a seat on a bench. Gran tells me the truth about my mum. She had wanted to tell me before, but Mum had forbidden her from speaking to me about it.

I have two sisters and a brother. The girls are six and four and the boy is two. She tells me their names but it is too quick for me to remember them. I think one was Ann or Annie.

She then explains everything to me. Everything. She tells me who my dad is. Not his name, but where he was from and what his job was. He was from Donegal, in Ireland. Mum was a young shop worker, nineteen, when she met him. She only went out with him a couple of times but that second time she got pregnant and he disappeared shortly after, presumably back to Ireland. She knew his name and where he was from but nothing more.

Mum had me, but she was on her own, and they all decided that the best thing to do was to put me into care. They heard about the Homes and agreed it would be a good place for me. She gave me up at three weeks old and Gran said Mum became ever so sad; for long afterwards she wouldn't speak to anyone.

Eventually she met a man and they got married and had a baby girl. Gran says that Mum's intention was to bring me back into the family once she had a family of her own, and that's what she still wants to do, but the time isn't right as the children are so young and I am doing well here.

She also says that the reason Mum is how she is when she comes to visit me is that she finds it very hard, as she wants me back, but she can never tell me that as she doesn't want to get my hopes up in case she can't make it happen.

I don't cry. I want to cry again but I don't. But it is nice to hear Gran say that Mum actually does want me back.

It's good of Gran to finally explain things; she says she feels I am old enough to know the facts. She says that she had thought I was old enough to know for a while now, but she didn't want to go behind Mum's back. But after the last time I saw Mum, she told Gran that it was time to tell me the truth.

Gran says it is a huge relief to finally be able to tell me and she says how sorry she is not to have been able to speak about it before and that she hated having to keep it from me.

She is such a nice lady, my gran. She has a kind face, and her eyes are warm and caring. When I fell out with Mum my only worry was that I wouldn't get to see Gran again.

I think you can tell that she is my gran. She looks a little like me even though she is much, much older and her face has more lines on it. Jonesy has met her and she says I look like her. Actually, she says I would look like her if I had been in the bath too long.

Gran asks me about Jane's murder, whether I've heard anything. She didn't know about Sally Ward going missing and that she is still missing. It's been four days now. She's got to be dead; everyone is assuming she's dead. Someone would have seen her by now if she wasn't. Gran is horrified at the thought of it. I tell her about Mrs Paterson's speech at breakfast and about her saying that life is much harder for women than for men.

When I say this, Gran looks at me for a long time. I think she is trying to work out how to reply.

Eventually she says, 'Life is different for women. It's not necessarily worse, just different.'

She pauses. 'No, it is sometimes worse, but only in some ways. Some ways it is definitely worse to be a woman, there is no doubt about that, but in other ways it is better, and I think that when you are a woman it will be a better time to be a woman than it has ever been before. But it is never easy, and it is often hard.'

'Was it hard for you, Gran?' I ask.

'Yes, Lesley, it was hard for me, but life is hard for all of us. There's no getting away from it.'

'What about for film stars?' I ask.

'It's hard for them, too. Just because they're famous doesn't make their life perfect.'

'So what should I do, Gran?'

'Just be you, my girl, and if you stick to being you, I am sure you'll be fine.'

I don't know what she means by that, but it seems nice and I feel good when she says it.

I tell her a little more about Eadie and she is happy that I have someone like her here for me. Then she has to go. Her bus is coming soon and she has to get home.

'Is your husband a good man?' I ask before she leaves.

'Who, Francis?' she says, then breaks into a smile. 'Yes, he is a good man; he's not perfect, but then no one is, and I think I made the right choice in marrying him. I'll tell you all about it one day.'

With that, she gives me a big hug.

She waves goodbye and I go back to the cottage with too many thoughts chasing each other round my head.

27

Jonesy has got in trouble. I worry as she can't help getting into trouble sometimes. She tries really hard to stay away from it, but then she will find some way despite herself to slip up.

I've tried to help her but you can't. She's a good person, there's not an ounce of nastiness in her. I worry that there's a part of her that can't help pulling her in the wrong direction, even if she wants to go the other way. I don't get in trouble that often, and when we are together it doesn't happen that much because if I can stop her I will.

She got caught with a bag of sweets. Got a dozen off the belt.

It wasn't her who stole them. She was given them.

The Homes has a general store to buy things from. It sells supplies for the cottages like food and milk and we regularly get sent there by Cook to get her things. It also has sweets we can buy, as we get a small amount of pocket money each week, plus I occasionally have money from

Gran. She is not supposed to give me money as some children don't have grans or visitors so it's unfair, but many times after she has visited I will find some coins in my pocket that she has slipped in when I wasn't looking.

Some of the older boys worked out a way to get into the shop when it was closed. They climbed up a pipe, stepped onto a ledge and got in through one of the back windows. They were going in every night for the last week; they waited until lights out, sneaked out of their cottages then climbed in and took some sweets. They were clever about it; they only took a few so that the adults wouldn't notice. If they had taken all the sweets in one go an adult would have figured it out straight away.

It was the McAdam brothers who did it – well, definitely one of the McAdams was involved. They are in Cottage 13, or unlucky-for-all if you live with them. It's away over the other side of the Homes. They have another sister besides Glenda, Angela, who is in Jonesy's class; she's less big and less crazy than the rest of them. She gave Jonesy some of her share of the sweets, as they are sometimes friends, so it's not even like she stole them herself.

Eventually someone realised that kids had been stealing from the shop so the houseparents were told to search everyone's bags after school and anyone with more than two sweets was going to get the belt.

Jonesy had far more than two sweets. It was obvious. Mr Paterson gave her a dozen.

When I come home from school she is crying in our bedroom. She tells me what a bastard she thinks Mr

Paterson is and how he really whacked her. She shows me her bum and it's beaming red. There is blood in two parts. Jonesy never really swears, none of us girls do, but she's right, he's a real bastard when he's got that belt.

Jonesy's lying on the bed on her front so she doesn't have to sit down. She says she thinks Mr Paterson enjoys doing it. Mrs Paterson could have done it, but she didn't.

I often think he hates us littler ones, especially Jonesy and Eldrey. Perhaps that's why the Patersons never had kids, as they can't handle them. He can deal with them when they are bigger; maybe they are not as annoying then. Mrs Paterson doesn't like the bigger ones and their 'teenage drama', as she calls it.

I know what Jonesy is talking about. He's used the belt on me before. I got back from school late for tea. It wasn't even my fault; the bus had broken down. We had to wait by the side of the road for an hour for another bus to come.

I had chores I was supposed to do that day, to help with the washing, and I missed them. When I got in the kitchen he just said, 'Beaton – THREE.' That means you are getting three lashes with the belt. He then wrote it down in his notebook. He writes it down like a to-do list of who needs to get them and how many. He will either do it on a Saturday all at once, or if it's really serious, like it was with Jonesy today, he calls you into his study and does it straight away.

I had to wait three days until the Saturday. I tried to tell him that it wasn't my fault, but he didn't want excuses. He said if he let me off then it wasn't fair on others, which means he *did* know it wasn't my fault and he was going to do it anyway.

I told Mrs Paterson and she said not to complain about her husband and that it's harder than you think to keep the house in line, so just accept it. I did accept it, I didn't complain, doesn't mean it wasn't wrong. He didn't even give me light stripes, but big whacks, ONE-TWO-THREE.

I can't bear to think how bad twelve must hurt.

Jonesy's face changes. 'I'm gonnae get him one day,' she says. 'I'm gonnae get him and then he'll be sorry. I don't know how, but I'm gonnae get him back.'

Sometimes her face gets so serious that she looks crazy. When she goes like that there's nothing you can do but agree with her. I've tried arguing before but if her face is like that there's nothing that's going to get to her.

'Aye, sure you will,' I say, nodding.

'You don't understand, Les. If I says I'm gonnae do it, I'm gonnae do it.'

Shona and Eldrey come into the room. They see Jonesy with her bum in the air lying over the bed and they can see she's been crying. They had been talking on their way in but as soon as they see her they go quiet.

Then Eldrey says, 'Belt?'

'Uh huh.'

'Whit for?'

'Sweets.'

'From the shop?'

'Uh huh.'

'The stolen ones?'

'Uh huh.'

'Angela McAdam got it too.'

'How d'you know?'

'Moira Campbell told us.'

Moira Campbell is in Angela's cottage.

'Aye, she got ten,' says Eldrey.

'Ten?' asks Jonesy. 'But I got twelve.'

'Aye, but no off the Superintendent ye didnae.'

Jonesy's right, Mr Paterson's a bastard. The Superintendent is a bastard and he's a bastard. Mr Paterson *can* be nice to you, though he tries his hardest not to be. Mr Gordon isn't nice to anyone ever; I don't think there's a nice bone in his body.

Jonesy lets out an 'oooffff' sound and she starts to smile. Which makes me, Shona and Eldrey smile.

That might be the one lesson I've learnt in the Homes; no matter how bad it gets, there's probably someone getting it worse.

28

They've found Sally Ward.

She's dead.

Two boys found her in a river about two miles from the Homes. She was wearing a summer dress. The boys had been fishing when they spotted her, tangled up in the reeds and lifeless.

Mr Paterson announces this news at breakfast. I know something is up as he held me back from leaving for school at my usual time and told me to get a later bus. We are all eating and he's been standing by the door waiting for everyone to come in before he taps an egg cup with a spoon to get us to be quiet. We know it is something bad. He only ever does something like this if it's bad news.

His head is bowed and his voice is shaking when he starts talking. I've never seen him so upset. 'I'm sorry to have to tell you all this, but Sally Ward's body has been found by the river. It was found yesterday afternoon and it appears that she may – and I repeat *may* – have been murdered. The police will have to confirm this.'

There is a big intake of breath. Even though that's what we had thought had happened, we still get a big shock that she is actually dead.

Jonesy says something like, 'Oh God.' I can't say anything. I feel dizzy. I didn't know the girl, but for a moment I think I might vomit on the floor.

Mr Paterson then says, 'Now, obviously this is a very disturbing thing to happen; we wanted you to know the facts before any rumours start. We are going to keep the curfew in place. Don't be afraid, but be careful.'

There is more silence. No one wants to be the first person to start talking, and no one wants to be the person to start eating or pick up their cutlery. How can you have breakfast when you have just heard something like that? We all sit trying to work out what to do next.

Eventually Mrs Paterson breaks the silence. 'Eat up,' she says. 'This is terrible news, but you've all got to have breakfast or you won't make it through the day. Come on, now.'

We slowly begin to eat, and kids start speaking, but only in a whisper. Most look stunned. One of the older girls is crying and another is comforting her.

*

After we finish, we run up to our bedroom. 'Jesus. Jesus. Jesus,' is all Jonesy keeps saying.

It is too shocking. Sally has definitely, definitely been killed. Why else are you dead by a river unless you've been for a swim – but why would anyone swim in that mucky cold river? No, she's definitely been killed. We all agree about that.

Two dead girls in a month. It is the most scared I have ever been. Also – and I don't know why – but I am excited, I think it's just that the news is exciting. It is massive, massive news, the second most shocking thing that has ever happened here after Jane being killed.

I have to get ready for school and catch the bus. I usually like to go to school but right now I want to go to the Homes school with everyone else and talk all about what has happened.

'Tell me anything you find out,' I say to Jonesy as we say goodbye. 'And stay safe.'

'You too, Les.'

*

When we get back to the Homes in the evening, Jonesy is waiting for me on the porch of the cottage. She isn't allowed out to wait for me by the gates any more.

It turns out that the Homes school was cancelled for the day, which Jonesy said drove Mr and Mrs Paterson crazy as the kids were all in the cottage and not allowed to go out. Mr Paterson gave numbers to four girls and put them in his book, for doing nothing. He's going to have a whole morning of whacking them this Saturday. Surprisingly, Jonesy wasn't one of them.

They can't cancel school again tomorrow. They can't have no school and no one allowed out of their cottages, it just makes the houseparents angry.

Jonesy says she heard that Sally had been strangled. Apparently, her neck was really red and her eyes were bulging out when they found her. She doesn't tell me who told her this, so I don't know if she knows this is true or if someone told someone who told someone who told Jonesy.

'D'you think someone had sex with her?' she says.

'How can you tell?' I ask.

'The polis will know; they can just tell.'

'How?'

'They look in their fannies.'

'Eugh.'

I eat in the kitchen while Jonesy fills me in on what's been happening. At tea they had a minute's silence for Sally, then they weren't allowed to talk during the meal.

After I eat, we run upstairs to our room. Everyone is on Jonesy's bed again. I sit on my bed and listen to them talk about Sally.

By the time the lights go out we are convinced there is a madman out there who wants to kill the girls from the Homes, and if we aren't careful we will be next. We don't tell ghost stories as we are all terrified enough as it is.

We ask Mrs Paterson if we can sleep with the light on. She says no. We all wail and she says she will leave the door open and the landing light on and if anyone is scared they can come and see her.

I have never known the Homes to be this collectively scared. The older girls are really worried, as whoever it is seems to be targeting girls their age. There is a lot of noise coming from their room and Mrs Paterson tells them to shut up. The truth is the killer could be after anyone. But as Gran said, life is harder for girls. I decide to go and see Eadie tomorrow, even though it's not my normal day. I don't think she'll mind after what has happened; she will probably have a queue out the building.

29

The next day kids at school still want to speak to us Homes kids because of the murders. It's terrible, but it means more people are talking to me and I think I have a new friend – Clara Dee. I knew who she was before, but she never spoke to me at break time as I kind of stood on my own in the playground, or did my homework in a classroom so I wouldn't have to do it back at the Homes.

She invites me to come talk to her and her friends to tell them all I know. I feel really bad because they are all listening to me and I make out that I knew Jane really well and that she was a proper friend of mine and that I am upset, so they put their arms round me to comfort me.

I know what I am doing is wrong, but they just seem to want to know more and more, so I just kept telling them things. They ask a question and I answer it with something, even if I don't know the real answer. The more I say the more they keep talking to me and the nicer it feels.

I have never been that bothered about being popular as I am just happy to be at the grammar school, but to have them be so interested in me gives me a feeling I like. To have a group of friends is the most wonderful thing.

*

On the bus on the way home Amanda tells me that Mr Taylor has been released by the police as they don't think he did it. He couldn't have murdered Sally Ward as he was in a cell when she was killed. She says she heard her houseparents talking and apparently they had ruled him out as Jane's killer already but Sally's death confirmed it.

She says he's not going to be coming back to the Homes, and that a lot of girls are disappointed. Turns out it wasn't just Jonesy who had a big crush on him.

I walk back to Cottage 5 to drop off my things before going to the hospital, and find Jonesy sat on the steps. She looks happy to see me and comes running up. I tell her I am going to see Eadie, and she looks sad, so I say, 'I'll come and find you as soon as I am done,' which cheers her up a little.

'What do you talk about?' she asks.

'Anything.'

'Anything? But you can talk to *me* about anything.'

'Aye, but this is different. She's just really nice to talk to.'

'Can she tell you who killed Jane and Sally?'

'I hope so, then I can stop being scared.'

'Scared? You don't have to be scared, Les. If you can beat that beast Glenda, you can beat anyone. You smash them with the gate and I'll kick them in the peanuts.'

30

When I get to the hospital building, I walk past a boy from Cottage 14 who has clearly taken a beating, and up the stairs, and take a seat outside Eadie's room. There are two boys there ahead of me, but they don't take long. I have spent a great deal of time sitting outside Eadie's room and I can tell you that boys take far less time than girls in there. I don't know if they have fewer problems, or if they tell her their problems quicker.

After half an hour the second boy comes out and Eadie appears in the doorway and beckons me into her office.

'Ahhh, the lovely Miss Lesley Beaton,' she says. She is wearing a twinset. I never knew what a twinset was until I met her ('How come your jumper and cardigan are both the same colour, miss?'). She's the only person I've ever seen wear one. This one is fawn with black trim. Her skirt is black, her shoes are black. You can see, like everything else in her life, she thinks about it.

'Miss—'

'It's Eadie, Lesley, you know that.'

'Those deid girls, Eadie, is someone tryin' to kill us? Does someone want all the girls deid, Eadie? Does someone want to rape us an' kill us? Why do they want to kill us and rape us? Do they rape us then kill us or kill us first? I would rather be killed first before I am raped, but I dinnae want either to happen.'

'Calm down, calm down,' she says. 'Now take a deep breath.'

'I wee'd my bed last night. No one knows because I took off the sheet and hid it in the cupboard then turned the mattress over. I never wee the bed. I don't want to be killed, Eadie.'

She gets up out of her chair and puts both her hands on my upper arms and holds me. She looks at me until I look back.

'Breathe slowly, Lesley, breathe slowly and calm down.'

I didn't realise how scared I was until I started speaking.

'Something shocking has happened, and it's natural to be scared, but let's look at things rationally. What has happened is rare – very rare. There is every chance no one else will be hurt. The deaths might not even be connected, it could just be a terrible, terrible coincidence.'

'Miss – sorry, Eadie – it cannae be a coincidence. Even I know that.'

'Maybe not, but it is rare. And you are safe and you are well and your friends are well, so let's not be afraid of things that we needn't be afraid of.'

'So there *is* a mass murderer? Like Peter Montrose?'

'We don't know, but you can't go around spreading panic, understand? I am talking to you as if you were an adult. You are a bright girl, Lesley, so I am going to treat you as such. Yes, it looks as though both girls were murdered. Yes, you should be careful, but no, you should not be scared. You can't spend your life being scared.'

'Yes, Eadie.'

'Now I want you to know that there are going to be police officers patrolling the Homes to make sure everyone is safe. People take your safety very, very seriously, so we won't let anything happen to you.'

'Yes, Eadie.'

'So what have I just told you?'

'Dinnae say nuthin' to no one, miss.'

'Now it's time for my question.'

'Yes, miss?'

'Is everything all right with you, Lesley? How have you been feeling about your family situation?'

'Oh yes, I ... I sorta forgot about it. I was angry but then my gran explained some of it, and with everything happening with Jane and Sally, I've been forgetting to be upset about it.'

'Well that's one good thing to come out of this.'

'Miss, that's naughty, you shouldnae say that.'

'You're right, Lesley, I shouldn't make jokes, sorry. But what I will say is, if you do get upset about it, you come and tell me. Yes?'

'I will.'

'Right, on you go.'

With that I get out of my chair and smile as I wave goodbye. Then I leap down the stairs and run back to the cottage to Jonesy.

When I leave Eadie I always feel like I have a new coat of paint on me. I go in feeling tatty and run down and I come out feeling ready to face the world with my bright new colours.

31

We are to be interviewed by the police today. They have come to our cottage. Mrs Paterson told us at breakfast they would be coming and before we had finished eating there was a knock. Shortly after, one of the officers put his head round the kitchen door to get a look at us. As soon as he did we all went silent. When he pulled his head back we all started talking again.

There are four policemen in all. They each take a different room in the house and we have to go to one of them and have him ask us questions. We all line up, then Mr Paterson tells us which room we have to go to.

I line up with Jonesy in front of me. She gets all excited while we wait. Four other girls get spoken to first, then it's our turn. Jonesy's policeman is in uniform, quite young, a little bit handsome. When she is told to go to the reading room where he's asking girls questions, she lets out a muffled, 'Yus!'

I go to the kitchen for my interview. My policeman is the only one not in a uniform. He is older than the others, maybe forty or fifty. His hair is parted on the left; it is slick and combed back and to the side. When I walk in, he points to the chair I am to sit in, then he lights a cigarette and starts another page on his notepad. He goes through a series of initial questions, like name, age, how long I've been here. He writes all my answers down with a super-fast scribble.

I'm not sure why he wants the last one. I was going to ask him how he thinks that might help, but when I look in his eyes, I can see he is someone I'm not going to help by asking questions, so I keep quiet.

He takes a big draw on the cigarette and on the exhale says, 'Right, my name is Detective Boyle. You know why we are here: to find out what you might know about these two incidents and where you were at the time they happened.'

'I will help any way I can, sir,' I say, making an effort to talk posh. I tell him I will help in any way I can, but I am not telling him about the diary or that it was us that sent the letter. That would get us in trouble and I don't want us in trouble, and I don't want us getting the belt.

'Did you know Jane Denton or Sally Ward?'

'No. Well, I knew who they were, but I didn't know-know them. I mean, Jane lived here years ago, but I mean *years* ago and she wouldn't remember who I was as I was only wee then.'

'Have you seen either of them with anyone they wouldn't normally have associated with?'

'No,' I say. 'Can I ask a question?'

'Aye.'

'Is it a mass murderer?'

'I can't answer that.'

'Cos me an' Morag Jones think there's a madman on the loose. Like Peter Montrose.'

'And why is that?'

'What if they hanged the wrong man?'

'They didn't.'

'But how do you know?'

'Trust me.'

'Why?'

'Because I'm a policeman.'

'And?'

'And because, young lady, I saw the evidence. I saw the evidence, I saw the man's eyes, and I saw them hang him by his neck. He killed those women, and he's dead, and I'm glad he is. Do you understand?'

'Aye, sir. But, sir ...'

'Yes?'

'Was it no Mr Taylor then, sir?'

'What do you mean?'

'They took Mr Taylor away a few days ago. Then Sally Ward died and now Mr Taylor is free, so you must think it's no Mr Taylor who did it?'

'No, it's not Mr Taylor who did it.'

'Not even Jane Denton?'

'No.'

'How d'you know?

'Because we eliminated him as a suspect. Now, this is supposed to be me asking the questions, not you.'

'Sorry, sir. We're just scared thinking that someone's

trying to kill all the girls in the Homes. So if it's not Mr Taylor, then there's someone free to do it again.'

He pauses for a moment. 'I think there might be an extremely disturbed individual who we need to catch. We can't confirm whether the two deaths are linked; all we can do at the moment is investigate what has happened.'

'Can we help?' I ask.

He seems to decide that I have nothing more to tell him. 'You can help, young lady, by keeping yourself safe and making sure your friends stay safe. Now, send the next girl in.'

As I come out Jonesy is already waiting for me. We go upstairs to our bedroom to find out what the other girls were asked. It turns out Jonesy can't remember what she was asked because she was too busy staring into the eyes of the policeman, who is, according to her, 'beautiful'.

I tell her what my one said about Mr Taylor, and what he said about Peter Montrose, and how he'd seen him hanged.

'Aww ... gross,' she says.

'I think we need knives,' I say.

'Do you think?'

'Aye, we need to protect ourselves if we get caught by the madman. We need sharp ones. We'll steal them from the kitchen.'

'When?'

'The sooner the better. Tonight.'

'Deal.'

32

First, I feel the breathing on my face, then I hear the whisper.

'Les, you awake?' says Jonesy.

I am warm under my sheets. I don't want to come out, but unfortunately this was my idea. 'What time is it?' I ask.

'Dunno. Too dark to see. It's late or early.'

I slip out from under the bedcovers. I have my pyjamas on and I went to sleep with my socks on so I wouldn't have to put them on in the dark.

'C'mon, let's do it,' Jonesy says.

We walk softly across the bedroom and she opens the door. It creaks, so she nudges it just a little bit more. The landing is dark and the house is in complete silence. We go down the stairs, sticking to the side so the steps don't creak. We cross the hallway and I feel the cold of the tiles through my socks, then we open the door to the kitchen. Again there is a small creak from the hinge when the door is pushed. We slip inside.

We can see a little clearer in the kitchen as the light from the streetlamp outside bathes the room in a slight yellow glow. The drawers in the kitchen dresser are big, so if you are going to ease one out quietly you need two people to do it. I point to Jonesy to go to one handle and I take the other.

I am just about to tell her to pull when we hear someone exhale, a sudden, 'Urrrrrrggghhhhh,' from behind us. Jonesy and I freeze. Mr Paterson is sat with his head resting on the table, with an empty bottle of whisky in front of him. He is fast asleep.

Jonesy looks at me and I look back at her. She must be thinking the same as me, which is, if he wakes up and catches us we are beyond dead, but also, we've come this far, do we go through with it and try to get the knives?

Mr Paterson breathes out again. He is silent for maybe fifteen seconds then lets out a huge breath. I am not sure how he is breathing in, as he only seems to be breathing out.

Jonesy nods at the drawer; she thinks we should go for it. I shake my head and point towards the door. She shakes her head and nods at the drawer again. I try to do my angriest face; there's no way I am going to get the belt again.

She shrugs and agrees. We look at Mr Paterson. Jonesy holds her hands up as if to say, 'Why?'

We reverse out of the room and go up the side of the stairs again and I slip back into bed. Jonesy slides in next to me. 'Whit was he doing?' I whisper.

'He's a drunk,' she replies.

'But the grown-ups aren't allowed alcohol in the houses.'

'He hides it. I've seen it in cupboards before. Some of the boxes under the sink have bottles in them. He must wait until everyone has gone to bed before he drinks it.'

'D'you think he heard us? D'you think he opened an eye?'

'Naw, he looked blootered. It's what grown-ups do.'

'Whit about Mrs Paterson?'

'Whit about her? She must know.'

I don't know how long we kept talking but Jonesy stayed in my bed for the rest of the night.

*

When it's time to get up and go down to breakfast on Sunday morning, Mr Paterson is there eating his toast as if nothing has happened.

We both watch him, because he doesn't know what we know. Jonesy smiles and shakes her head and we both turn to Mrs Paterson to see if we can tell if she knows what her husband has been up to. But we can't tell.

33

Mum comes to see me in the afternoon. I don't want to see her. I don't want to be anywhere near her.

We usually sit in the tearoom and talk when she comes, but this time we go for a walk around the grounds. She is wearing her long dark coat, and her hair looks greasy and a mess. I don't think she is taking care of herself.

She doesn't try to hug me when she sees me. She just coldly says, 'Hello.' I reply with the same and try to put as little niceness in it as possible.

We set off walking down Faith Avenue, then go up Praise Road and around, via Love Avenue and Church Road back again – the full loop. We just walk together in silence. I am not going to break it, I refuse to. I don't have anything to say and I don't want to try to make her feel better.

We keep walking the damp roads until Mum finally says, 'I'm sorry, Lesley.'

I wasn't expecting her to say it, so I don't know what to say back. So I don't say anything.

'I'm sorry. I'm sorry I wasn't in a situation to be able to bring you up myself, but you being here is the best thing that could have happened to you.

'I really want you to come and live with us, I really do, and I will make it happen, just not right now. I've always wanted to be able to have you with us. When you were born, I couldn't bring you up, but now I have a proper home for you. I just need it to be the right time.'

I stay quiet. I can't seem to think of anything to say that would seem right, so rather than say anything wrong I say nothing. At least she said sorry, at least I know she wants me. She's never seemed like she wanted me before. She is not very warm or how you would think a mother should be with their child.

'Would you want to come and live with us if I could get my husband to agree to it?'

'Of course, but only if *you* want me.'

'Want you? Of course I want you. I've always wanted you, Lesley.'

She turns me round and holds my hands. There are tears in her eyes as she tries to speak. I am still determined not to cry; I am not going to show her I care. I can't, I can't care, I can't let her in.

'Lesley, I want you so much, I want you to come and live with us and be the big sister to your brother and two sisters. It might take time, but never think that I don't want you to be with us.' She squeezes my hands. 'It's just we can't right now, but one day.'

With Mum there's always an, 'It's just ...' I believed her up until she said that. But now I remember everything else she's ever said that has never come true. Things she's promised in the past, times she's said she'd come see me and not turned up.

If Gran says she'll come, she comes. If she says she'll bring something, she brings something. If she says she'll do something, she does it.

I'm not sure how she could have given birth to Mum, nor how I can be related to Mum. I'm like Gran – I always do what I say I'm going to do.

When Mum was saying sorry, I had started to believe her. I really wanted to. But those two words make me think of all the times she's let me down. I stop listening to her for a while. I realise I don't look like her, so I must look like my father, whoever he is. I don't act like her, so I wonder if I act like my father too. I wonder if he even knows I exist?

I start listening to her again, but I realise they are just words. Only words.

'I was so worried when I heard about that second girl getting killed. I couldn't stop thinking about you. Are you kids scared? I saw the polis at the entrance. How is your friend? Are you looking out for each other?'

I stop listening again.

We walk some more. I let her ramble on.

When it's time to go she gives me a squeeze and says, 'We'll be together soon.'

It means nothing.

When I walk up the steps to Cottage 5, I don't turn back to look at her before I go inside.

34

Seeing Mum always makes me feel worse. I never feel happier after she's been, unlike when Gran comes. *She* never fails to make me feel better. The next time I see Eadie Schaffer I'll ask if she can arrange it so I don't have to see my mum for a while. She can do that and put a block on visits if I need it.

After my chores I go upstairs, get into bed and pull the blankets over my head so I am hidden. I don't cry. Mum can't make me cry any more. If I don't believe her promises, then she can't let me down or hurt me. You can only be hurt by people you care about. The only person I care about is Jonesy and that's how I am going to keep it. The smaller the number of people you love the smaller the number who can let you down.

The other girls come into the bedroom and start talking. They don't see me under the bedclothes. They're talking about a boy at the Homes school. Does he like one of the girls, does he not, does he like someone else? I don't know the boy they're on about.

One day I am going to escape this place. When I am seventeen I will get a home of my own, probably with Jonesy. We will get jobs, we will get money, we will have a life where people don't give you the belt for doing nothing wrong, where people don't try to fight you because you are cleverer than they are.

I think we will move to Paisley or Glasgow. Maybe Glasgow, as it is bigger. One thing for sure is that when I leave here I will never come back. Or if I do come back it will be in a big black car with a driver. I will drive through the Homes but I will not get out of the car. I might wind the window down a little but not too much.

The call for tea goes up. I can't face talking to anyone else today so I stay in bed. Jonesy pops up to see if everything is all right. I tell her I'm fine but that I just want to be alone. She says she'll bring up some bread rolls for me.

Then Mrs Paterson comes up. She's obviously asked where I am. I tell her I am fine and that I didn't enjoy seeing my mum, so I want to stay in bed for the rest of the evening. She seems all right with this, but says she will bring up a plate of food as I need to eat.

She also says that this is a one-off and I am not to do it again; if I agree to eat my tea and not do it again then she will leave me alone.

35

That night Jonesy gets out of her bed, crawls across the floor and gets into mine.

'Budge up,' she whispers. I move over and she gets under the blankets. 'Know what I've been thinking, Les?'

'Usually never.'

'We can sort this. And we *have* to sort this, find out who killed Jane and Sally, otherwise we might be next. The polis dinnae know whit goes on round here, not really. That means we've got a head start. You could work out who did it. You just work out who knows them both and it's probably them, right?'

'Not necessarily.'

'No, not necessarily, but still probably, aye? If we found out who could have done it, Lesley? If we found that out, we could work it out?'

'Mibbie.'

'Aye, mibbie. And mibbie I could sleep in here with you tonight?'

'Away yerself.'

'But I'm scared, Les, I'm s-s-s-scared and you can keep me safe.'

I know she's joking but I let her stay. Sometimes I let her stay, sometimes I don't. The benefit of her staying is that it's nice and warm and there's someone to hold. The problem is it's a bit squashed and she gets 'the jumps' in the night. This is when for no reason she suddenly starts to jerk in a dream, and it wakes you up, but never her, and it drives me crazy.

She falls asleep quickly. I lie awake for a while wondering who knew both girls, and that if they struck again it would be bad for the Homes but easier to work out. That is a horrible thought; the more girls die, the easier it should be to find out who killed them.

Are we bait? Is that what the police do, wait for something like this to solve itself by letting more people die and getting more clues?

This is my last thought as I fall asleep.

36

Bedlam this morning. Shelley McDade – one of the big girls from our house – has gone missing.

We are woken up, as always, at 6.30 a.m. by Mrs Paterson ringing the bell. I hate that bloody bell. I was having a dream and she ruined it. We all get dressed in our room while Mrs Paterson gets the babies up, then the next thing there's a panic from the big girls' room.

The big girls' room is down the end of the hallway. There are six of them in there and they are aged fourteen to sixteen. They give us so much trouble if we ever go into their room, but they can come into ours whenever they like. They often take things and threaten us with a 'doing' if we tell on them.

Anyway, Shelley McDade is gone. Her bed isn't made; she has just *gone*. She went to bed last night, then when everyone woke up in the morning she wasn't there. It doesn't seem as if any of her clothes are missing.

I go cold. The thought that anyone could come into

our house and take one of us without anyone noticing makes me pure terrified.

Mrs Paterson and Mr Paterson are frantic, they're looking everywhere they can in the house. Cook comes up to help. They keep searching in the same places, as if Shelley might come back in the time since they last looked. We just stand on the landing watching them racing about.

'Stay in your rooms!' shouts Mr Paterson.

We go back to our bedroom and Jonesy sits on my bed with me. Shona and Pam sit with us. Eldrey is on her bed, silently looking at the floor and shaking. Mary is as scared as anything. She keeps walking backwards and forwards repeating, 'Oh no, oh my God, oh no, oh my God ...'

Mary really likes Shelley. We all seem to have one of the big girls who we like. Mine is Fiona Manning. She always keeps an eye out for me. She's a wee bit cannier than the others, which is why I think she likes me.

'Whit have they done with her, whit have they done?'

Pam gets up and peers out the window. 'Shit, it's the Superintendent,' she says.

We all rush to the window.

'Oh my God, he looks like he's gonnae murder someone,' says Jonesy.

'He does an' all,' says Pam.

Mr Gordon storms up the cottage path and bangs on the door. Someone lets him in, and we go to the bedroom door to see what's happening. We open it a little so we can just see down the stairs.

'What the fuck is going on?' he shouts.

Mr Paterson is trying to calm him down and tell him what has happened. It's strange seeing Mr Paterson – who can be a bastard – be intimidated by an even bigger bastard.

We hear bits of their conversation. Mr Paterson says when they last saw Shelley, what happened when they went into her room this morning, who her friends are.

The Super asks if the police have been called. When Mr Paterson says no, the Super shouts, 'Well, why the fuck not?'

Mr Paterson gets on the phone, then the Superintendent starts to march up the stairs. We shut our door but can hear his boots coming up. He opens our door and looks in. We all hold our breath, then he shuts the door. He goes on, opening every door on our floor.

'Holy shit,' says Jonesy.

'I know,' says Pam.

'Look! Look!' shouts Mary. 'It's her, it's her, it's Shelley!'

We go to the window and it *is* her. She's walking up to the cottage carrying a towel.

'Oh, she is so deid,' says Pam.

We don't have a chance to go and tell anyone before Shelley opens the front door and walks inside. We all run to the top of the stairs again. Mr Paterson turns around and puts the phone down. He sees Shelley, walks up to her and before she knows it – SMACK – she's on the floor – sparko.

None of us says a word. Mr Gordon comes out from

the last bedroom on the landing. He walks through us and down the stairs.

'That her?' he asks Mr Paterson, pointing at Shelley on the floor.

'Aye,' says Mr Paterson.

'She all right?' the Super asks.

'She won't be when I'm done with her,' says Mr Paterson.

The Super doesn't say anything, just nods and steps over her body and leaves the house.

Mr Paterson sees us all at the top of the stairs. 'GET BACK IN YOUR ROOMS AND STAY THERE TILL WE CALL BREAKFAST!' he shouts.

We do as we are told.

I had been feeling very sorry for myself. If Shelley has done nothing else, she has managed to make me stop feeling so bad. But I worry for her. She's in for an awful day.

37

At breakfast we are told that we all have to go to the Central Hall again. I tell Mrs Paterson that I will miss the bus and miss school. She says I have to go and that she will try to get Mr Paterson to drive me to the school afterwards to make up time, but if that isn't possible I will have to work on my own in the cottage. She says that missing one day of school won't kill me.

Jonesy and I walk hand in hand from the cottage to the hall. Standing room only again, although this time it is only the girls who are here. The other girls are scared, I am scared, Jonesy is beyond scared. She's been having nightmares for weeks now. That's probably why she's been coming into my bed more than ever. It is as if she thinks I am going to be able to protect her from them.

In the hall everyone is trying to work out what we have been called here for. Is it about Shelley? Has another girl been killed? Have the police caught whoever murdered Jane and Sally?

The hall is bare when we walk in. It's used for lots of

different activities, but when there's one of these meetings everything is cleared to the side and the chairs and tables are stacked. It's a cold morning – especially for this time of year – so most of us have our coats on and we don't know how long we are going to be in here so we don't take them off.

Mr Gordon walks onto the stage. Jonesy squeezes my hand.

'Ladies,' he says, then a moment later, 'LADIES!' until we are finally silent. 'Thank you.' He looks around the hall. 'You all know what has happened here over the last few weeks, and I understand that you are alarmed by this situation. That is natural.'

Him trying to be kind and compassionate is even more unnerving than when he is a straight-out psycho.

'What I want you all to know is that you are very safe at the Homes. There are many responsible adults here, so if you are at all worried, speak to a grown-up.'

This is just what he said before, when Jane died. I feel suddenly cold. If he is just saying the same things, then he doesn't know any more than he did and we are not any safer. He is supposed to be in charge of the Homes, so if he is just saying words with no meaning then we are helpless.

I see Eadie Schaffer at the side of the hall. She doesn't see me as she is facing the stage.

'This is a tough time,' Mr Gordon goes on, 'but the police are on the grounds and the Chief of Police has called me personally and told me that they will catch this person. That said, we can do more to protect ourselves, so for now, I want you all to continue to go about in pairs at all times. Plus we are going to be handing out whistles to all of you girls. These will be delivered to your cottages this afternoon. Most importantly, be alert; if you spot something you think is suspicious, tell an adult. There is no harm in being wrong. It's better to be safe than sorry. Together as a community we will get through this and things will return to normal.'

'What, beatings and beltings?' whispers Jonesy.

No one else hears her but I nudge her anyway.

I want to ask Mr Gordon if there are any suspects, or who the police think might have done the murders, but the Superintendent doesn't ask for questions. I think of putting my hand up to ask anyway, but I don't want to draw attention to myself.

He ends with, 'Dismissed.' There is a scrum at the door at the back of the hall as we all try to file out at the same time.

'They havenae got a clue who's done it, have they Les?' says Jonesy, as we get into the fresh air. 'If they did, they would give us some idea that they were close to catching them.'

I think she is right, but I want to calm her so I say, 'They might no want to alert the person they think did it.'

'Nah, garbage, Les. They don't have a clue. Like I've been saying, it's up to us to find out who did it. Not for them, for us, so we can be safe. If we find out who did it, I'll be able to sleep normally again.'

'You might be right, Jonesy.'

'You know I'm right, Les. The polis have got their job to do catching bad guys. I've got my job to do stopping people raping and killing me. It's gonnae be my number one priority.'

'You off to school now?' I ask.

'Aye, you?'

'Going back to the cottage. I've missed the bus but Mrs Paterson says Mr Paterson will run me over to the school and if he doesn't I'll have to stay at home.'

'Oh, you lucky bleeder. I wish I could have a day at home.'

'Really? I like school, I'd rather be at school than at the cottage.'

'Aye mibbie at your school, no ours, no way.'

Jonesy is convinced my school is some wondrous happy place and everyone is a brainiac. Neither of these things is true. Even at a school like mine there are people who are cleverer than others. I just try to keep up. Some of them are super-clever, though. There's a boy in the year above me who is a certified genius. He walks strange, like he's walking up a hill and leaning into it at an acute angle. That's my favourite angle, by the way. I like an obtuse angle, but the acute angle is my favourite. I like the look of it, I think it's a cute angle. That is my best maths joke. Jonesy has never got it, but I like it all the same.

38

The cottage is always quiet when everyone has gone to school. The babies usually make a bit of a racket, except when it's their morning nap. Then there's a numb silence. But as I get closer to the house, I hear Mr and Mrs Paterson shouting inside. They don't tend to shout that much at each other, at least not compared to some houseparents. Over in Amanda's house, Cottage 9, apparently they row all the time, and sometimes one of them goes away for a few days.

Mr Paterson comes out of the house. He looks angry and is breathing through his nose.

'Get in the car,' he says shortly. I haven't done anything wrong but he clearly doesn't want to take me to school.

The car is a dark green. It has two doors and the seats fold forward if you need to get in the back. I don't know the type of car, I'm not that interested in them. Some of the boys my age are; they still play with toy cars like they are children, even though they are twelve. Football and cars occupy their minds; they make them happy. Like a dog playing with a ball. I think in a couple of years they will wake up and realise there are girls all around them, and pay attention to us, but at the moment a lot of them don't even know we exist. *We* know *they* exist; they don't see us.

I get in the front seat. I've never been in Mr Paterson's car. In fact, I haven't been in many cars – I get buses or trains or walk – so getting in one is a treat, or it would be if someone more cheerful were driving. And I've never been in the *front* seat of a car before. I am excited and scared.

Mr Paterson starts the engine and we drive out of the Homes. I am not going to say anything to him, it will probably only make him angrier, so I just look out of the window at the passing fields and hope he doesn't start shouting at me. It's not my fault the Superintendent called the assembly and made me miss the bus.

After five minutes he actually speaks. 'So how are you feeling, Lesley? I hope you're not too scared with what's been going on?'

'It's no nice, Mr Paterson,' I say. 'Why would someone do something like that to Jane and Sally?'

He stares at the road ahead. 'Unfortunately, Lesley, there are some bad, bad people in the world.'

'Like Peter Montrose?'

'Aye, like him. He was a very bad man, and that's why they hanged him. How do you know about him?'

'I heard what he did. He raped and murdered women, didn't he?'

'Yes he did, but he's gone now.'

'Whit if they got the wrong person, Mr Paterson? Whit if Montrose wasn't the killer?'

'They didn't hang the wrong person, Lesley.'

'But whit if—'

'Lesley!'

I look down at my shoes. They are black lace-ups. I try to keep them as clean as I can because the teachers can pull you up on them if they are scruffy. The sole on the left one is starting to wear away near my big toe and sometimes water seeps in if it is a wet day.

'You do feel safe, don't you, Lesley? You know you have grown-ups around you that you can trust. We won't let anything happen to you.'

'Aye, Mr Paterson.'

We carry on driving. I thought he was just going to drive me to the train station, but we go all the way into the town.

We are about two minutes away from the school when I say, 'Mr Paterson, me and Jonesy are going to find out who did it. We'll work it out and then we'll all be safe.'

'You do that, Lesley, you do that,' he says, but he doesn't sound convinced.

I get out of the car and Mr Paterson drives off. I try to open the school gates but they are locked. I don't know if they lock them to stop people getting in or to stop kids getting out. Luckily after ten minutes it is first break and a teacher comes into the playground and lets me in.

My new friend Clara Dee wants to know why I am late, and wants all the latest news about what's going on at the Homes. I tell her, and I make it sound as exciting as I can. We go to the spot in the playground where we hang out now, dodging the rampaging boys.

When the bell rings we have to go to separate classes, but we agree to wait for each other in the dinner hall so we can sit together. I feel terrible for a moment, for thinking *I hope this excitement continues*, as it will mean Clara will still want to be my friend. I know I shouldn't think this, but sometimes it's hard when you have been on your own in the playground so often.

39

When I get back in the evening all the girls have been given whistles and are standing outside the cottage on the grass. Jonesy had got one for me and rushes up to hand it over. We are not to blow them under any circumstances – except if we are in danger, of course – so after about half an hour everyone starts blowing them. Some of the boys have made it a game to steal them off the girls and run around blowing them.

I can see why we have been given whistles; the grownups weren't to know how silly the boys would be. I'm sure they'll get bored of it and they'll be used properly by tomorrow.

I tell Jonesy about the car trip with Mr Paterson. I tell her what he said about Peter Montrose, how he's definitely dead and that the policeman had said that too.

'They *would* say that,' says Jonesy. 'They just want us not to be scared.'

'Aye, but if it's no him, then who is it? It could be anyone.'

We walk back to the cottage. Mr Paterson is stood in the doorway, but he doesn't say hello or acknowledge us, so we just walk past him into the kitchen. I sit down to eat the tea that Cook has left out for me. Cook is still there, tidying up.

'Get yer whistles?' she asks.

'Aye,' we both say.

'You keep them with you, aye?'

'Aye,' we both say again.

You don't want to mess with Cook, she has knives and a temper. We always do whatever she tells us. Jonesy isn't scared of many people, but she is scared of Cook. Cook's forearms are like the giant hams we get at Christmas. Sometimes when you budge past her you can feel how strong she is. If she were a man, she'd be a soldier.

I eat my tea while Jonesy talks to Cook. I realise if someone else is going to be next it's not going to be Cook. No one would stand a chance with her. I need to be more like her, but people are never going to fear me, I just don't have it in me.

40

After I've eaten, Jonesy and I sit on the steps and look over towards the duck pond. I don't know why it's called the duck pond because no ducks ever come to it. Boys occasionally get thrown in it especially if it is their birthday. 'Dunked pond' would be better.

'We need to catch him. We need him to be put in jail or, better still, hanged,' I say.

'Could you do it?' asks Jonesy.

'Do what?'

'Hang him. If you knew it was him and you had to pull the lever, could you do it?'

'Aye.'

'Aye, me an' all. Would that make us killers?'

'Not until we've done it.'

'Aye, so we're potential killers.'

'We're all potential killers, Jonesy.'

'I think you are more of a potential killer, Les. I think you would do it and no give it a second thought. I think you would be reading your book, reach up, pull the lever and then go back to reading.'

'Give off.'

'You would, Les, you're a stone-cold killer, so you are. I'm keeping one eye open at night from now on.'

'I could never kill you, Jonesy,' I say. 'I need the sound of you talking to get to sleep every night.'

'You'd still hear me talking. I'd come back and haunt you and widnae ever let you sleep again.'

41

I tell Jonesy I'll see her back at the cottage and head for the Homes library. One of the things the founder believed in – apart from the sanctity of the word of the Lord, which would bring salvation to us children of sin – was that education would be another saviour. So the library is huge.

I love the library. I'm not a big one for stories, but I love facts, and books have lots of facts. I can read the encyclopaedias from cover to cover. I'll read anything that I can learn from. They also have old newspapers. Other children have used the newspapers to find out why someone's dad is really in prison. Today I want to read about the Peter Montrose murders. They scare me, but I need to know all the details.

I ask the librarian where the papers from ten years ago are. She asks what I am looking for and I say I am looking up articles from around the time my little brother was born. From then it is just a case of forwards and backwards with the papers. There was nothing at the end of the year, but at the start they mention Peter Montrose had been caught. In the middle of the year they hanged him, but I want the reports from the trial so I can find out what exactly he did.

He murdered eight people. It's a relief to find out that it wasn't just young girls he murdered; he murdered older women too. Reading the transcripts from the court it seems pretty certain that they got the right man. The doctors said he was a psychopath, he had no compassion, and if he hadn't been caught he would have killed again.

*

I go back to the cottage. Jonesy is upset that I didn't tell her where I was going. I only went without her because she would have got too excited in the library and would have been unable to keep her mouth shut. Libraries are supposed to be quiet and she wouldn't have been able to cope.

She seems disappointed that it really couldn't be Peter Montrose killing Homes girls. I love Jonesy so, but sometimes she's a bit too crazy to keep up with.

We do our chores and then go to our room. Jonesy gets out an exercise book and shows it to me. She's already started to put together a list of suspects. She points at Suspect 1.

'It's the da of Glenda McAdam.'

'Away,' I say.

'No, true. You look at it, Lesley, look at it. You add the

bits together and it comes back to him. You've seen him, aye?'

'Aye.'

'He's an evil-looking man.'

He is an evil-looking man. He's been in Barlinnie countless times. When he turns up at Cottage 13, you know about it. He has four kids in the Homes. Their mam is rumoured to be a drunk or a whore or both, but no one ever dares say it to them. Maybe that's why Glenda and the brothers are like they are. It can't be nice having parents like that.

'Well guess whit, Les, I heard the big girls talking yesterday and Jane Denton had a run-in with Glenda McAdam two months ago. Lots of kids at school are saying that Jane and Sally were friends, though no close like you and me, more like me and Brenda, so mibbie Glenda hated Sally too. And more, Sally Ward went out with one of the brothers, but then just split up with him, and then like two days later she's deid.'

'So why would it be the dad? Why wouldn't it be the brother?'

'Aye, right enough, Les, but anyway the brother doesn't look evil enough. The da would, though, he'd strangle a puppy for eating a sausage.'

'Away, Jonesy.'

'It's true, Lesley, and you could be next. You duffed Glenda, it could be you that's going to get done now.'

'Dinnae say that, Jonesy.'

I feel sick. It could be Mr McAdam. He is a bad man. He has a reason, even if it is not a good one. The bad parents, the really rotten ones, are not supposed to come to the Homes, they are banned. But no one can stop him from turning up when he wants to see his kids. There aren't any adults strong enough to kick him out and usually one of the houseparents has to call the police, but by the time they arrive he is already gone.

Some people hate the police, but imagine if that is your job, you turn up and you've got to get rid of someone like him. I wouldn't want to do it.

Even though I doubt it is him, he is someone to keep an eye on. After all, Jonesy has a point – he *is* capable of it.

42

I have had an amazing day at school today. I get pupil of the week. I've never got it before. The pupil of the week gets to wipe down the blackboard at the end of Friday's lessons. Mrs Andrews says I have been working incredibly hard. I *have* been working hard, but no harder than I usually do. I don't know why she chose me this week in particular, but things seem to be going better for me now that I am friends with Clara and we have our own set of friends. I would have felt awkward being pupil of the week if I wasn't friends with them, as I could have been teased, but now that I am it makes things a lot easier.

For dinner we have jam sponge and custard, which I love, and Richard Metting smiles at me as we walk down the corridor. Some days it just all goes for you, and some days it goes against you. Sometimes I think it doesn't matter what you do, it just happens like that, but mostly I think the harder you work, the more likely it is to work out for you.

Life's funny like that. I might have not worked hard and all three of these things could still have happened.

When I get on the bus to go back to the Homes I almost don't want to. I don't want it to be the weekend, because that means it is two days until I get to come back here. Still, I am happy.

Ever since the time us four Homes pupils sat together, I've been sitting in the middle of the bus, where I can hear what the older ones are talking about. And I was right that as boys get older they get more into girls. Today Daniel and Ronnie are talking about a girl with breasts at school; they are trying to use better and better words to describe them: 'amazing', 'immense', 'science-defying'.

Amanda is saying how pathetic they are. Ronnie says that jealousy is a lousy trait in a woman, which makes Daniel laugh. Amanda looks hurt, but she tries to pretend she isn't. If I've learnt anything at the Homes, it's not to let them know when something they say affects you. If they spot it, they can get at you, and that will make it worse. It's hard to do and if even Amanda Bell can't do it, and she's one of the most impressive girls around, then the rest of us have got no hope.

The boys continue to tease her until she shouts, 'Oh, grow up,' and turns around to face the front. I am peeping back through the seats to see her and she catches my eye. She shakes her head, not at me, but at what she has to put up with. One day I would like to be her friend.

The bus stops at the Homes. As Ronnie walks past Amanda he has his fists up his jumper to make it look like he has giant breasts, and he says, in a high-pitched voice, 'Oh, bye, Mandy, have a nice weekend,' and walks away like a girl. As we get up to leave the bus I almost speak to Amanda; we have a moment, a look, but I don't, I am too shy, and she's too old for me to really talk to.

I walk towards my cottage, regretting that I didn't take the chance to say something, when I see a big crowd standing outside. I walk through the crowd, trying to get to the front steps.

As I do, I hear Kelly McDowell say, 'She's here,' and I see Eadie Schaffer is stood on the porch. She rushes towards me and gives me an almighty hug, repeating over and over again, 'I'm so sorry, I'm so sorry.'

'What is it?' I say. 'Why are you so sorry?'

'It's Morag,' she says. 'She's been killed.'

43

I don't speak to anyone for a week. I can't get any sound out. I shut down.

At times my body won't move, and I can't make it move. I am no longer there. I watch people talking to me but can't hear them. I can't eat. I sit in my room a lot.

They talk about putting me in the hospital but Eadie argues that I need my home environment. It is decided I will stay at the cottage and that Eadie will visit me in the morning and evening and sometimes at dinner as well.

They keep me off school for a couple of days, but that doesn't help, I have nothing to do, I sit frozen, with people asking me if I am all right and do I want tea. I have never been offered as much tea in my life, as if tea will help bring Morag back.

Jonesy was strangled. They didn't tell me at the time, just that she had been killed. I hear later that she was strangled. She was found on the back steps of our cottage. I can't go round the back of our cottage as I worry that if I see the steps I will see her body.

Cook found her. Cook is also too distraught to talk. She will cook food but she won't speak. They offer her time off, but she shakes her head and points to the kitchen.

From what they have said it sounds like Jonesy fought and fought. I know she would have. She had so much life in her and she wasn't going to give that up without a struggle. No one has said if she was raped. I don't want to know if she was.

44

The days go by as if I weigh two tonnes; it feels so hard to move my body anywhere. I wake up every morning and my first thought is, *I am awake*, and then there's five seconds before I remember what has happened. I think, *I wonder if Jonesy is awake, or if she's going to come into my bed*, and that's when I remember and that is when the sadness comes. It's so heavy, and I can feel it all over my body. And I just want to go back to sleep because when I am asleep I don't know she is dead, but when I am awake I do know, and I know I will never see her again and then I start to cry.

I don't know what to say to anyone. The only thing I can think is that it's so unfair. I could think of a hundred people more deserving than her to die.

Eventually I start to talk to people again. At first to Eadie, then to the girls in my room. The girls in my room are sad too, but they hug me and hold me tight. Mrs Paterson often comes up to check how I am doing.

At breakfast one morning Mrs Paterson comes and sits

next to me. I'm eating my porridge and trying to avoid eye contact with anyone.

'How are you today, Lesley?' she asks.

'Alive,' I mumble.

'The police would like to talk to you this morning, if that's all right with you? They've talked to everyone else in the house but they'd really like to talk to you as you were Morag's best friend.'

'Fine.'

'It doesn't have to be now if you don't want, you can take your time.'

'Right.'

'You don't have to do it on your own. I can come with you, or Mr Paterson, or Eadie—'

'Eadie,' I say.

'Right, I think she will be on her way over anyway so if you go to your room after breakfast, I will let you know when she and the policeman get here. If you want to go to school afterwards, Malcolm – I mean Mr Paterson – can run you up there in the car, but by no means do you *have* to go to school.'

I don't tell her that I want to go to school; I like it at school, when I am in the house I have nothing to do and can't stop thinking about Morag and crying again, which makes them think I am still not ready to go back to school.

I haven't been in my room long when there is a knock at the door and Mrs Paterson comes in.

'Eadie and the policeman are here now,' she tells me. 'If at any time you want to stop talking to them you just let Eadie know, and I will be about if you need me.'

'All right,' I say.

I walk down the stairs and Eadie is stood by the front door with a man. He's much smarter than the other policeman; he's wearing a long brown coat, a hat and shiny shoes. As I get to the bottom of the stairs he takes off his hat and smiles at me. His face is very thin, and his parted brown hair is a bit of a mess from the hat so he smooths it down.

Eadie gives me a big hug. It feels good. She makes me feel safe.

'Lesley, this is Detective Walker,' says Eadie. 'He's come to ask you some questions about Morag, to get a better picture of her, as no one knew her better than you did. If you could help him by answering them, I am sure it would be really appreciated.'

He crouches down and looks at me eye-to-eye.

'I know this is going to be really hard for you, Lesley – is it all right if I call you Lesley?'

I nod.

'I should introduce myself. As Miss Schaffer says, my name is Detective Walker. I'm thirty-seven years old. That's very old, isn't it? How old are you?'

'Twelve.'

'Twelve? So I am three times as old as you.'

'And remainder one.'

'I'm sorry?'

'You are three times as old as me with a remainder of one.'

'You like maths?'

I nod.

'It sounds like you might be better than me at it.' He looks at Eadie who nods as if to say, 'You are probably right.'

'Anyway, I am Detective Walker, and if you want to remember that, it's because in this job I have to do a lot of walking. See my shoes?'

He shows me the bottom of his shoes and they are nearly worn through on the soles.

I smile a little. I don't mean to, but I can't help it. He's talking to me as if I am a baby, but I don't mind. He's just trying to be friendly, I can see that.

'So I am thirty-seven and I have been a policeman for seventeen years, which, knowing you, you will already have worked out how long I was *not* a policeman for.'

'Twenty years,' I say.

He nods. 'All right, Lesley. I know it will be hard, but it would really help me and the other policemen trying to find who did this if we get as much information about Morag as we can.'

Eadie suggests we go sit at the dining table. As we go through, the detective takes his coat off, then the suit jacket he has on underneath. He puts them on a chair as Cook comes to see if she can get us any drinks.

Eadie and the detective ask for a coffee. I ask for an orange squash.

Detective Walker sits down, gets out his notepad and pen and says, 'What we are looking for, Lesley, is background. Anything you can tell us about Morag would be useful, any detail you can think of. How long you've known her, was she happy, did she have any enemies, who were her friends, all this information could be vital.'

I nod understanding, and Eadie suggests I start by telling him how long I have known Jonesy, and what room she was in.

'I've always known Morag. We call her Jonesy as that is her surname, Jones.' I realise straight away I said 'is' instead of 'was'.

'We've both been in Cottage 5 since we were three and I dinnae remember before then, so as far as I can remember I've always known her. She slept in the junior girls' room in the bed next to me. She was always my friend, my best friend, we did everythin' together, other than school as I go to a different school. Even then she would sometimes come and wait for me to get off the bus when I came back in the afternoon.

'She was a fidget, a real fidget, quite often she would go to bed in my bed and it was always really hard to get to sleep because she would twitch when dropping off and she was even worse when she went to sleep. She would go still, and then suddenly jump like she was being attacked.

'She loved her doll, Maggie. It's so manky, but she always had it with her when she went to sleep. She would bring it into my bed. It's in my bed now. She hated having it cleaned, but it had to be sometimes, as it got horrible. She left it in my bed the night before she died and I will be able to keep it, won't I ?'

'I'm sure you will,' says Eadie.

'Good. So she was lovely and bubbly and she had lots of energy, and she wanted to do everythin'. And she was so nice and why would anyone want to do anything to her?'

'Did she have any enemies?' Detective Walker asks.

'Naw. I mean, not really. There were people who didnae understand her, thought she was a bit out there, a bit crazy, but not anyone that properly didn't like her. Not like me. People don't like me cos I go to the grammar school. If anything, they'd ask her why she was hanging out with *me*. No, people liked her even if they found her a bit much.'

'Sure, sure,' the detective says.

I look at him. I really look at him. What is he thinking? Is he trying to work out if someone thought she deserved it?

'And what did she think of the other incidents?' he says.

'You mean the murders?'

'The other deaths; was Morag scared?'

'She was scared, we all were, but also excited.'

'Excited?'

'I know, she was a bit crazy, but any big news made her excited. She wasnae perfect but why would anyone want to kill her?'

At that point I catch Eadie's eye. 'Why would anyone want to kill her, Eadie?'

And then I start to cry. Eadie gets up and puts her arm around me.

'It doesnae make sense,' I say between sobs.

'I know,' says Eadie, 'I know.'

'I'm so sorry,' says Detective Walker. 'When I was your

age, I had a best friend called William. We were insep-arable. But he caught pneumonia and died, and I just couldn't understand it, how someone who was always there wasn't there any more. I knew old people died, but I had never known anyone young die, and he was only ten. And I couldn't help thinking how and why, and I had to fall back on my faith that God would have a plan—'

'But if God has a plan,' I say, 'why would he have a plan to kill Jonesy? That's just rubbish, that's a rubbish plan.'

'We may not know why he does what he does,' the detective says.

'Well if he does know then I hate him and I don't want anythin' to do with him.'

'Don't say that,' says Detective Walker.

'Why not? Whit's he going to do, kill me too?'

'All right, I think we'll leave it there,' says the detec-tive, and he gets up and puts his jacket and coat on. He tears off a piece of paper from his notepad and writes a number on it next to the name 'Frank Walker'.

'If you can think of anything that might help us, feel free to call us any time at the incident room. Ask for me and if I'm not there leave your name and number and I'll call you back.'

He squats down again, puts a hand on my arm and looks me straight in the eye. 'Lesley, we are going to do everything we can to get whoever hurt Morag. We have many people working on this, and we are going to find that person and they are going to be punished. I am not going to rest until they are caught. You have my word on that.'

I thank him and he gets up and leaves. I am left in the dining room with Eadie. After a few minutes of silence she leans over and says, 'You did well, Lesley, you did really well.'

I force a little smile. 'Why *would* God do that, though?' I ask her. 'No one will explain why. If I ask the minister, whit will he say?'

'I don't know, Lesley, everyone has their own opinion when it comes to religion.'

'And whit's yours?'

'It's not for me to say, my view is personal.'

'Why won't anyone give me a proper answer?'

'Because the answer is different for everyone, Lesley; the answer depends on what you believe.'

'All right, so I am asking what do *you* believe?'

'I don't.'

'Don't what?'

'Believe … in the whole God thing.'

'You think it's made up?'

'Yes. I'm more science- and fact-minded.'

'But that's whit I sometimes think. I thought that before, and that's whit I was thinking now, cos, like, why would God do something like that and anyway how would he do it, and like, no one has ever seen him? It must be made up.'

'Who's to say what's right? But listen to me, Lesley, this is very important: you must not tell anyone what I've just said. Religion is very important at the Homes and I would be out of a job, immediately, if anyone found out. Do you understand?'

'I understand.'

Mrs Paterson comes into the room and I go a little red as it feels like Eadie and I are talking about something top secret and I think Mrs Paterson can tell.

'Let's go for a walk,' Eadie suggests, and we go off round the grounds and have the most amazing talk, like she is talking to me as if I am a grown-up, which no one ever does. If it were possible it only makes me think more of her. She doesn't think what people tell her to think, she thinks for herself. I vow to myself that from now on I will do that too.

45

In the afternoon I'm told to go to see the minister. Mrs Paterson says that as I have so many questions about religion and why God let Jonesy get murdered, perhaps I should go and talk to him. The minister, not God. I guess that Detective Walker must have told Mrs Paterson what I said about God. I wish he hadn't.

I walk up to the church on the hill. The clouds are a muted grey and the drizzle lands lightly on me. Not enough for a full coat but enough that when I arrive there is a gentle covering on my cardigan.

I push the church door open. It's heavy and it takes both hands and all my weight to push it open far enough for me to squeeze through.

Candles are lit at the front and as I walk up the aisle I see Mr Samson stacking Bibles. He must have heard the door but it isn't until I am within a few yards of him that he turns round. He has a bald head like a chess pawn and a long black cloak. He greets me by taking my hands and clasping them in his, putting his forehead against them.

He gives me the creeps. He's been to the cottage a couple of times to console me and I have tried to avoid him each time. I didn't want to come, but Mrs Paterson insisted.

He invites me to sit with him in the front pew.

'I gather you have some questions,' he says, bending his head down as if to get a proper look at me.

'Naw, no really,' I say, hoping I can make this encounter as short as possible.

'Now come on, Lesley, there's no need to be shy. Mrs Paterson has told me about your questions, about God and so on. It's good to ask questions.'

I don't answer. I have become better lately at holding silences. I never used to be able to, but if Jonesy's death has taught me anything it's that I don't have to talk to anyone. They can't make me.

'My child, do not be afraid to share your thoughts. It shows you have an inquisitive mind. God values that.'

'Does he?'

'Of course he does. He wants all his creatures to think about the wonder of the world.'

'Does he want us to question whether he exists?'

'He knows people will question their faith at times.'

'He does? And what does he say to them when they do, because I'm thinking that he doesnae actually exist. For one, if he were to exist and control everythin' then why let whit happened, happen to Jonesy?'

'Our faith will be tested many times in our lives.'

'So you're saying God has decided to test my faith by killing my best friend? That's no right, is it? I don't think he's sat about and said, "I know whose faith needs testing, Lesley Beaton's. And the best way to test her faith is not by doing a miracle, or making a vision appear, but by having Morag Jones murdered." That doesn't seem like a test a normal person would set, and if it *is* a test God would set, then he's clearly some sort of crazy.

'By my reckoning there are two options: he does exist and he's a brutal, unhinged murderer, or he doesnae exist, and all this is just made up like Father Christmas and there really is no one in charge, so we are all just fending for ourselves. But then if he doesnae exist why would everyone go to all the trouble of building big churches to worship someone imaginary? They can't be lying to everyone, can they?'

The minister takes my hands in his again. I just want to scream, 'LET GO OF ME!'

He speaks in a calm, low tone. 'God has many paths for us all, and we do not know why he chooses each path, but we have faith that the path he has chosen is the right one. And though we may question his ways, or even his existence, we know that he loves every one of us.'

I pull my hands from his. 'That doesnae answer my question; that also suggests he loves the person whit killed Jonesy, which goes back to my first point about him being crazy.'

'You have been through a lot, and it is only natural for you to question, but know that God will be there for you when you need him.'

'All right,' I say, giving up. I think if I sat here for a week he still would not be able to give me a straight answer. I decide to be polite. 'Thank you for your help.' I get up and walk back down the aisle.

As the sound of my footsteps echoes round the church he calls out after me, 'The Church is always here for you.' I lift up my arm as if to say thank you, but as I walk out I think the truth is, there is nothing for me here and I have just learnt the biggest secret of my life, that grown-ups lie, a lot, and the Church is the biggest lie of all. Father Christmas multiplied by a hundred.

The thing I can't figure out is, why would they do that? What's in it for them?

46

The next day is the day I have been dreading. I have to finally say goodbye to Jonesy.

This is the first funeral I have ever been to; only Jane and Sally's housemates went to theirs. I have never known anyone die, even old people. I am in a fog. I feel like I am walking in a giant balloon and everyone is looking at me to see how I am, and I don't *know* how I am.

They won't let me be on my own. If I go for a walk someone always walks with me and asks me how I am, and they keep saying I should talk about it, I should say what I feel, but I don't know what I feel and I don't know how to say it, and so I don't say anything. At mealtimes I feel everyone watching me. I want them to stop but I can't bring myself to say anything, so I just keep my head down so they can't see my face.

It feels like when you've been slapped hard on the ear and there's a ringing sound that goes all over your head for about ten seconds. I feel like that ringing is going on all the time. I physically feel as if I've been hit and am struggling to stand up.

And now it is the day of Jonesy's funeral, and there is no one here from her family. I don't know if they've even been told that she has died.

The whole house gets up in silence this morning. Even breakfast is eaten in silence. Everyone is dressed in black. It's Saturday so the others from Cottage 5 are held off school for the funeral. Everyone in our house is going, as well as her classmates.

The girls in our room keep crying. We all keep crying, and when two people are crying another person will join the group and cry, and others will join in and it never seems to stop.

For the last week I have had her doll Maggie in my bed. I gave it away last night so they can put it in the coffin with her. I wrote a letter for her and sealed it and asked them to put it in too. I will not tell anyone what was in the letter, it was personal, and when it's my turn to go I hope I meet up with her and we can discuss it.

'It's here,' comes the call from downstairs. Not 'she's here', but 'it's here'. That means that the hearse has pulled up outside our cottage. I don't look out the window to see it.

'C'mon,' says Shona, and she takes my hand and leads me downstairs. The front door is open and it's at that point that I see the car and the coffin in the back. I think for a moment that it would be nice for Jonesy to be able to come inside for one last time, but she can't.

Mr and Mrs Paterson are stood behind the car and

there are others standing behind them, all dressed in black. Mrs Paterson holds out a hand for me to join them and I walk along the path to the road. I try not to cry but I can't stop myself. I get to Mrs Paterson and she holds me close to her. Mr Paterson rubs my head, and my tears and snot go all over Mrs Paterson's black coat.

I try to wipe off the mess I've made. 'It doesn't matter,' says Mrs Paterson, and I grab hold of her gloved hand.

Mr Paterson gives a nod to one of the undertakers, who gets in the car and starts driving very slowly. We walk behind it down Faith Avenue and then right onto Church Road all the way up to the church.

Everyone is silent; the only sounds are the low rumble of the car, and feet on the tarmac.

When we get to the church we don't know if we are supposed to go in first, or the coffin. Eventually Mr Paterson tells us all to go in. Mrs Paterson walks in with me still holding my hand and we sit in the front pew. Mr Paterson comes and joins us. I cry some more. I want Shona, Mary, Eldrey and Pam to join us but they sit in the row behind me. Shona and Mary are white in the face, and Pam looks a bit sick. Eldrey has her eyes closed and is praying hard. She is the most interested in God out of all of us. Maybe she thinks he'll stop her getting the belt so much. I put my head down, alone between the two adults.

When everyone has sat down, they bring in the coffin and put it up on a stand. It's level with us, *she* is level with us. She is in that box, dead.

That thought stops me crying.

The minister gets up to his lectern and starts to speak. I can't hear what he's saying. After our talk I have little interest in what he has to say anyway, it's all just lies.

I think about Jonesy. Our bedroom is so quiet without her. I think of how the space her personality used to take up is now not being taken up by anything, nothing fills it, it is just empty space. I think about how it is all so unfair. She didn't get to grow old; someone took that from her.

The one thing I don't feel and haven't felt is scared. When Jane Denton and Sally Ward were killed, I was scared, but now I just don't care. If someone is going to kill me, then let them kill me.

Mr Paterson gets up to speak. I try to listen to him but cry some more. I hear some bits about 'being there for each other', and, 'Morag loved life, and we must hurt but then heal.' Neither bit makes much sense to me. Then he looks directly at me and says something about 'the twins', meaning me and Jonesy.

When it's over we stand around outside. Pam, Shona, Eldrey and Mary join me and we wait for them to bring out the coffin and put it in the car to take it to the graveyard.

She is getting buried in Paisley as Renfrewshire Council have requested she be put there and they are the ones paying for it. There's not enough space at the cemetery of the Homes church, not unless you're very important, and apparently Jonesy isn't important enough.

Mr and Mrs Paterson and I get in the back of a black car. There is a bus laid on to take the others to the graveyard which is about twenty minutes' drive away.

We ride in silence. I stare out of the window and see grey clouds hovering above us all.

When we get to the graveyard we walk up to the hole in the ground. This is where Jonesy is now going to stay for ever, all on her own.

Mr Samson says prayers as they lower Morag into the grave.

We stand around until it's time to go back to the Homes. I decide to ride on the bus. I sit with Pam and Shona and they cuddle me all the way.

Back at the cottage there is food laid on. The Superintendent is there, and Mr Paterson introduces me to him. Mr Gordon already knows who I am, though he has never spoken to me before. He shakes my hand with both of his; the light comes off his shiny bald head and he smiles at me. His smile looks sinister. He might be trying to be nice, but I can't feel the kindness; he's always terrified me and him being nice is just as bad. His teeth are yellow and his skin is red and stretched, like he has been boiled.

'I understand you were good friends with Morag Jones.'

'Aye, sir, we were best friends.'

'I'm sorry for your loss,' he says as he rubs my shoulder with his shovel-like hand.

'Thank you, sir,' I say. I am determined not to cry in front of him. In fact I am determined to get away from him as soon as I can.

'We will find who did this, Lesley, and we will punish them.'

He fixes me with a stare, like he is staring *into* me, like the inside of me must know that he is going to be true to his word.

I don't doubt it. If he finds the person who did it, he will punish them with his giant arms and giant hands. But then, the police didn't find the murderer after Jane or Sally died. How is this any different?

*

Around about two o' clock the mourners start leaving the cottage. Outside, boys are playing football as if nothing has happened. How can they still do that?

I go to my room and start to read. I am reading a book called *What Katy Did* at the moment. Someone bought it for me in the hope it would make me feel better. It's about an American girl who is a bit of a rebel. I like it but I find it hard to concentrate on the words as I drift off easily.

At tea that evening we have sausage and mash and thick gravy, which is my favourite. I think Cook might have made it especially for me. Mr Paterson says grace in the same way he has done every night since Jonesy died. He asks the Lord to look after her up in heaven and to look after us down here.

He doesn't know that I know that there is no Lord. And if there is no Lord there is no heaven. So Jonesy isn't in heaven, she's just dead. No happy place in the sky, just lying underground in the graveyard in Paisley, surrounded by other dead people in boxes.

I am glad the funeral is over because I couldn't do it again. It was a day I needed to get through. Now is the next chapter of my life, but I don't know how I am going to do it without Jonesy. I stop listening to Mr Paterson and eat in silence. A few of the other girls talk, but it's still very quiet. It's always quiet since Jonesy died.

47

I go back to school on Monday. Clara Dee is very nice to me. All of her friends are now nice to me too. They wait for me to arrive in the morning, and they save me a space at dinnertime.

At the Homes I just want people to leave me alone; at school I am glad people are being friendly. Even the teachers are really nice to me, they check how I am, and smile at me when I come into the class. I am not stupid, I know that they know, and I know why they are doing it, but I don't mind. No one treats me like the poor kid any more. It's almost as if I was just like one of them. It's horrible that it has taken something like this to happen for them to notice me.

Now I'm back at school I'm happier than I have been since Jonesy died and I think I know why. Jonesy was never here; she was never at the grammar school. There is nothing that reminds me of her. At the Homes everything I see reminds me of her. *That is where we sat together after she fell and cut her leg. That is where she had a wee behind the bush when she was desperate.*

The worst place is our bedroom. Being in there just reminds me of her non-stop. I've thought about asking Mr and Mrs Paterson if I could sleep in another room, maybe with the big girls, but then I realised I don't want to be away from Jonesy's bed.

Mrs Paterson's talked about them taking Jonesy's bed away. I said no straight away. I even slept in her bed one night when I couldn't get to sleep as I wanted to smell her.

They've given me a teddy bear, as if that would make up for the loss of Jonesy. He's called Albert. I am twelve years old and for some reason they think a teddy will help me. The strange thing is it really does help. I hug him when I go to sleep, and I like the feeling of him next to me, I feel like he will protect me. I shouldn't need a teddy bear but I can't help how I feel.

At school I work as hard as ever. At ten to three I know I only have sixty minutes left and I start to feel sick as I know I will soon have to get the train and bus back to the Homes.

I wonder if I should join a sports team so I can stay longer. There are teams that practise after school some days, but then I wouldn't be able to go back with the other Homes kids. I could ask Mr Paterson if he would come and pick me up, but I know what the answer would be. People are being nice to me now but that would be pushing things.

48

I come to a decision when I wake up. I decide not to be sad any more. I decide that I have a choice: I can either be sad about Jonesy for the rest of my life or I can do something about it. I can find the person who killed her, and I can make sure that they spend the rest of their life in jail or, even better, dead.

Every day that they are not caught is a day they are free and walking around, and I don't want them to be free, I want them to be in a prison cell feeling terrible for hurting Jonesy, or I want them to be waiting to be hanged and wishing they hadn't done what they did to her. I know you shouldn't want someone dead but I don't care. This person deserves to die for what they did to Jonesy and the other girls. If I can make that happen, I will. I am closest to all of this; the clues must be closest to me. If a man killed Jane and Sally, why would he kill Jonesy too? She had nothing to do with those girls. The older girls seem to have been friends, so that might be a connection between them, but they definitely weren't friends with Jonesy. I just need to work it all out. Jonesy thought I could.

I'll speak to Detective Walker again and find out what he knows. I didn't say much last time, but if I get him to come back to the Homes I can tell him what I know and he can tell me what he knows, and together we can work out who did this.

When I get to school, I go to the stationery cupboard and take a notepad, then I start writing down what I know about the murders. When Detective Walker comes I'll put down what he knows too.

I have a purpose. The fog has lifted and it is time for action.

49

'She's called Petal.'

'I know,' I say.

'Wannae stroke her?'

'Aye.'

I walk up to the caretaker and the horse and pat her on the side. Her coat is matted. It is a dirty brown colour with a splodge of white on her face.

Mr Sharples watches me pat her. 'Aye she's a biggie, sixteen hands,' he says.

'She smells a bit,' I say.

'Well, wouldn't you if you'd been pulling round this cart all day?' He points to the wooden trailer behind her, filled with hedge clippings. 'New here?' he asks. 'I havenae seen you afore.'

He has, he saw me before the fight with Glenda McAdam, but maybe I am just forgettable.

'Nah, been here since a wean. I dinnae go to the school, though, I go to the grammar school, so am not about as much as the others.'

'Wannae help me walk Petal back to the stables?'

'Aye, all right,' I say.

Mr Sharples is wearing dungarees with a stained light green shirt underneath. He looks dirty, like his face needs a proper wash. His grey hair is brushed forward like some men do when their hair is going thin. I don't know why they do it, Mr Paterson doesn't. His is trimmed but you are not to mention his lack of hair, as he can get angry about it.

'She's a great friend,' he says, 'and do you know the best thing about her?'

'Whit?'

'You can tell her all your secrets and she won't tell a soul. And we've all got secrets, haven't we?'

I nod.

We walk down Love Avenue and he lets me hold the lead-rope.

'She's sixteen years old, is Petal. Old enough to start courting, aye? You're still a bit young for that, aren't you?'

'Aye.'

'Give it time, 'fore you know it you'll be fighting them off, eh?'

I don't want to talk about boys. I stroke Petal's nose some more, and change the subject. 'What does she eat?'

'Mainly oats. It's nearly time for her tea so you can help me feed her.'

'All right,' I say.

We turned onto Church Road.

'I havenae even asked your name, young lady. What is it?'

'Lesley.'

'Aww, that's a lovely name. My name is Mr Sharples.'

'I know. You live over at the farmhouse just outside the main gate.'

'Aye I do, I do. And Petal here lives in the field out behind it. She has a lovely field to wander around in.'

'Is she lonely out there all on her own?'

'D'you know, I've never asked her that. Hey, Petal, do you get lonely in that field all on your own? I bet you dinnae; I bet you've got lots of other animals you are friends with.'

'How long have you worked here?'

'Twenty years now. I've seen them all come and go. So many of you youngsters, you're everywhere, and all growing up so fast.'

We walk to the farmhouse. He uncouples the cart and pulls it around the side, then comes back and says, 'I'm just going to get a bucket of feed from inside, you two stay here.'

'Whit if she runs off?' I say.

'Look inta her eyes, Lesley. She's tired, she dinnae want to run off. She just wants a bit of food and a chance to stop pulling this cart.' He goes inside.

I turn to talk to Petal. 'You wouldnae run off, will you? You are a nice horse, and a nice horse wouldnae run off.'

She lowers her head to me and I rub the top of her nose and her cheeks. He was right, she does look tired. Her head jolts up when Mr Sharples comes back out with her tea and she shuffles a little with her feet.

'Bring her round the back, there's a place where I hook up the bucket.'

I lead Petal round the back of the farmhouse and he fixes the bucket to a fence pole. Petal goes straight in with her nose and starts crunching away.

I think, *Here I am with Mr Sharples and Petal and no one knows where I am, and I am always supposed to tell someone where I am going and to be in a pair.* I feel a sudden slash of fear.

'I expect you've been pretty scared with all the goings-on around here of late?' he says.

'They killed my best friend.'

'Who was that?'

'Jonesy. Morag Jones, they killed her.'

He is silent for a moment and then says, 'I'm very sorry.'

'I'm gonnae catch them. I'm gonnae make them pay for whit they did.'

'I'm sure you will,' he replies.

'You dinnae believe me, do you? No one believes me, but I will catch them. No one does that to Jonesy and gets away with it.'

'It must be really hard.'

'It is.'

'D'you want a piece of chocolate?'

'I should be getting back to the house.'

'It's just inside. It would cheer you up.'

'Naw, I have to go, I have to get back, but thank you.'

'S'all right,' Mr Sharples says. 'Any time you want to come and say hello to Petal just come on over, she's great at helping you not feel so sad. She's saved me from feeling sad many a time.'

I wave goodbye to him and to Petal and walk back to Cottage 5.

*

When I get back, Pam is on the front steps with Shona.

'Where *you* been?' asks Pam.

'I walked Petal the horse back to the farmhouse with Mr Sharples.'

'The caretaker?'

'Uh huh.'

'Oh God, Leeeessss, whit did you do that for? He's a weirdy.'

'He seemed nice.'

'Les, he's a creep, he whistles at girls when they go past, did you no know?'

'Yeah, the way he looks at you is gross,' adds Shona.

'He was nice to me, let me feed the horse and offered me some chocolate.'

'Oh God, Lesley. It couldae been dangerous. He's strange, I wouldn't put it past him being the one whit's been doing it all. Jesus, Les, you had a lucky escape.'

'Getaway.'

'Think about it, Les. Who has keys to all the houses? Who can go anywhere in the grounds? Who would be the best person to hide a murder weapon?' says Pam.

'But—'

'He's no married, is he?'

'I dunno.'

'He's not. He's over forty and he's no married. Why not? Cos he likes young girls, doesn't he?'

'I saw the polis talking to him two weeks ago, before Jonesy.'

'They spoke to everyone.'

'I'm telling you, Lesley, be very careful.'

I feel bad. He was really nice to me, but they are right. Mr Sharples is a bit strange, I think, and I worry about him for the rest of the day.

50

Gran came to see me today. Eadie told me my mum knows about Jonesy. I'm angry that she hasn't come to see me herself. Neither her nor Gran came to the funeral.

Gran gives me the biggest hug when she sees me and she doesn't let go.

We go to the tearoom and she buys me chocolate cake and fizzy pop and tells me about when her brother died. He had a heart attack and just died in the back garden one day. She was doing the washing up with his wife when she saw him fall into the fence and then into the plants. They rushed over but he was face down in the soil. He had been turning over onions with the garden fork and his heart just gave out.

She talks about the days after he died. She says she felt numb and confused. She says there's no set time for grieving and in a way it never ends, you just get used to it.

Then she starts telling me a funny story about a lady who lives on her street who people thought was carrying on with someone who wasn't her husband. She has never really told me stories like this before, but I think she is trying to treat me like more of a grown-up. The woman was seen leaving her house at strange times and people had started to talk about her. Anyway, it turns out she was seen in Glasgow city centre, in a bar, and she was kissing another woman, and now everyone on the street knows this apart from the husband and no one will tell him.

The gossip makes a tingle go through me. My first thought is to go back to the cottage and tell Jonesy. I finish the cake and Gran orders another pop for me and another tea for her.

After that we go for a walk around the village. I have never walked so much in my life as I have since Jonesy died. Everyone wants to take me for a walk. I think it might be so they don't have to look at me while they talk to me.

We walk up to the bridge over the stream at the front of the Homes and stand there watching the water flow underneath.

'There are some very bad people in this world, Lesley, but don't ever forget there are some very good people too.'

I say, 'I think you were born a good person, Gran, and my mum wasnae.'

She looks at me, horrified. 'I'll pretend I didn't hear that,' she says.

'Why?'

'Because you don't know whit your mother has had to go through.'

'Well, why do you come to see me and no her? If she loves me, surely she would want to see me. You do, but she doesnae.'

'Your mother loves you very much, so much you'd never know.'

'I don't know because she's never told me.'

'Lesley, your mother loves you even if she's never said so.'

'That's the thing, Gran, I don't think she does. I can tell *you* love me. But I think a lot of talk about love is a way for grown-ups to keep kids quiet.'

Since Jonesy died I've begun to realise that grown-ups lie, a lot. They lie to try to make you feel better, they lie to stop you asking questions. They say, 'It will be fine,' when it most definitely won't be fine.

Gran's face changes and she fixes me with a glare. 'Now you listen to me, Lesley. I know you're having a hard time, but I will not listen to you talk like this about your mother. You have no idea how hard it is for your mum to not be able to be with you. Now, let's get you back to your cottage.'

We walk to Cottage 5 in silence. I feel so alive having said out loud what I have thought all this time. I have never said anything before, to keep people happy. Well now I don't care about keeping people happy. I am going to say what I think, and no one is going to stop me.

51

I haven't seen so many policemen about the Homes in the last few days. I wonder if they think we're safe now as nobody's been killed for a while. But that doesn't make any sense. They should only have fewer policemen about once they capture the murderer. I don't know why they haven't arrested anyone. Maybe they don't care about us because we are kids without parents, so they aren't bothered that we are being murdered. If it was outside they would care; someone's parents would make the police do something. But in here, nothing. They send some police around for a few days, ask a few questions and then go back about their business. How many more of us have to die before someone is arrested?

After school, I decide to go and see Eadie. There's no one waiting for her and no one in her office so I just walk in. She looks happy to see me. She's reading some papers but puts them aside when I appear and gives me a hug. She asks if I'd like a cup of tea and I seem to be getting a taste for it so I say yes. She says she was hoping I would come by as there was something she wanted to talk to me about.

I freeze. I immediately think it's something bad and I can't take any more bad news. She sees this and tells me it's nothing to be afraid of and she'll explain all shortly.

We go to the small kitchen near her office and while we wait for the kettle to boil she asks how my day was. I tell her about Clara Dee. I say I am becoming good friends with her – not best friends, as I will never have a best friend again, but definitely good friends. I tell her about what we are working on at school and the marks I've been getting.

She offers me a biscuit, which I take, and we go back to her office. When we sit down, she fixes me with a look and I know what she is about to say will be serious.

'How do you feel about adoption?' she asks.

I don't know. I don't know how I feel about adoption, so I smile and shrug.

'Because there is a couple who might be interested in adopting you. They seem like lovely people. Would you like to meet them?'

'I think so,' I say.

'You don't have to, you know.'

'I know. Well … aye, if you say they're nice.'

'They are. I think you will like them. I think they could be great for you.'

'I didnae think anyone would want to adopt a twelve-year-old. People want to adopt babies, not kids my age, once we've already gone wrong.'

'You haven't gone wrong.'

'Naw, that wasn't what I meant, I meant before we've got personalities.'

'Maybe that's true, but maybe there are people out there who don't want the trouble of bringing up a baby. Maybe there are people who think, *We don't have children, perhaps we could help someone who can be helped, who deserves to be helped*.'

'You think I deserve to be helped?'

'Lesley, I can't tell you anything, I can only guess at someone's motivations, and I can only suggest the child that would benefit most. I haven't put forward any other children to the couple. Do you see what I am saying, Lesley?'

'Aye ... I think so.'

'Good. Now, this isn't straightforward, adoption never is, but the first step is that you are interested. The second is whether your natural mother is agreeable. I hope you don't mind, but I have already talked to her and told her how good this could be for you and fortunately she has agreed in principle.

'The next step would be to arrange a meeting for you with the couple to see if you still want to go forward with it.'

By the time I leave to go back to the cottage I am excited by the idea. I am also scared; what if they don't like me? What if they are strange, or religious, or strict? Still, it'd probably not be any worse than being in here. Maybe something good will finally come of this summer.

52

On Saturday I am still thinking about what the girls in my room said about Mr Sharples. I decide to write down the facts.

Mr Sharples

- He is weird.
- He can get anywhere in these grounds without anyone suspecting him.
- He can carry tools that can hurt people and it not be suspicious.
- He could have been in the woods where they found Jane and just said he was after kindling.
- He could have driven Sally Ward's body to the river on the back of his tractor and no one would have noticed.
- Jonesy never liked him. Maybe she told him she thought he was a suspect?
- Being weird isn't a reason to be a suspect, you can be weird and not be dangerous, but he is weird.

- He was nice to me the other day, but maybe he was doing that for a reason, maybe he was trying to appear normal, because of what he did to Jonesy.
- No one seems to be doing anything about the killer. Why don't we matter?
- The police say they need evidence and if they aren't going to get it then I will. I will not sit around and let this happen to another girl. That girl could be me.

The murderer might not be Mr Sharples, but then again it might be, and anything I can learn about him will help, even if it means I can rule him out. I've never spoken to him before the other day, and he's never spoken to me before. But Pam said he whistles at girls when they go past. Maybe I'm too young so he *wouldn't* say anything to me; maybe it's just girls who have boobs he says things to.

Jonesy and I used to pretend we had boobs; we'd stick stuff in our jumpers and walk round the room like we were older. We even stole a bra from the big girls' room once, tying a knot in the back to make it fit properly. Then Jonesy pretended to be a boy talking to me who couldn't stop looking at my boobs. I smile at the memory of it, but as soon as I do I feel sad.

It makes me determined to do something. I'm going to go to Mr Sharples's farm buildings to see if I can find out anything about him.

Yesterday was the last day of school and it's now the summer holidays, so I have plenty of time to investigate him. I leave the cottage and walk around the village until I spot Mr Sharples, cutting the big patch of grass that runs along Praise Road. I know what I have to do. I walk fast through the gate and across to the farmhouse. I go straight round the back so no one can see me. I see Petal standing there in her pen, and wave at her. I remember what Mr Sharples said: 'The horse can't tell anyone,' so she can't let him know I've been here.

There's a large garage filled with tools and machines. I try the rusted red metal door and it opens straight away, but with a loud creak. Inside it is dusty and dark and the only light comes in through one dirty, dusty window. It smells of dried grass, mud and oil, and everywhere you turn there is equipment – a small tractor, a little motorbike; along one wall is a saw, a rack that has all sorts of screwdrivers and spanners on it, and some mallets.

If you wanted to kill someone there is plenty of stuff here you could do it with.

Along the same wall is a desk with a noticeboard above it, which has letters pinned to it. There's a wooden chair in front of it with a brown overall draped over the back.

On the desk are a radio, a light, and what looks like a small engine of some sort that Mr Sharples might be repairing. There are also some letters and envelopes spread out.

The desk has two drawers, which I open; in one is a pair of battered shoes, in the other is a folder, but it's just filled with receipts. I open one of the letters. It's from Renfrewshire Council, saying that 'after consideration' his job would be continued.

I open another; this one's from the Dykebar Hospital.

Dear Mr Sharples,
   I note with disappointment that you have missed your last two appointments.
   It is vital that you continue your treatment with us. To miss further appointments would not only jeopardise your health but also your employment as we would be duty bound to inform your employer.
   Please contact my office as soon as possible to reschedule an appointment.
   Yours sincerely,
   Dr H. Talbot

I can feel the heat in my face as I read the letter.
Shona and Pam were right – he's a mental.
The Dykebar is where the mentally wrong go. Some of the parents of Homes kids are in there; that's why they can't look after their children. And one of the older boys was sent there after he went crazy and started trying to attack everyone with a hammer.
I have to tell the girls. I have to get out of here.
Outside, I hear whistling and the sound of metal being rolled on the path. I drop the letter, run to the back of the garage and duck behind the tractor.
The door creaks loudly as Mr Sharples pushes it fully open. He's talking, but it seems to be to himself. I peep over the tractor wheel and see that his back is to me. He is stood at the desk, mumbling.

A bead of sweat comes down my forehead and rolls down my nose. I'm trying to breathe as quietly as possible. I watch as Mr Sharples pulls open one drawer, then pulls open the other one, then tuts.

My legs are starting to hurt. I'm crouched down and my thighs are cramping. He has to leave soon – I can't stay in this position much longer. Mr Sharples looks in the first drawer again and lets out a big sigh and then walks out, shutting the door behind him. The garage is now dark apart from the small patch of light coming through the dirty window.

I breathe out. I wait for what I think is five minutes, to be sure he's left, and then climb out from behind the tractor. I try the door handle but it's shut tight and won't open. I didn't hear Mr Sharples lock it. I lean against the door but I can't get it to move.

I look around for another way out and realise that the window is my only chance. I put a small stool underneath it, open it up and squeeze through. It's so tight the metal frame scrapes my leg as I lower myself down. I have to go head first and end up doing a handstand to reach the ground. Luckily, I'm good at handstands at gym, and I take a few steps forward on my hands before flipping over to land, a little stunned, in a crab position.

I get up and brush myself down. I shut the window as much as I can, then creep to the side of the building to make sure I can't see Mr Sharples. He's not there, so I walk as fast as I can back to Cottage 5.

When I get there, Shona looks me up and down. 'Where've yous been?' she demands.

'Nowheres,' I reply.

'Then why is your shin bleeding?'

'Fell over, didn't I?'

She thinks about it. 'You fall over on your knees, not your shin, you liar.'

I have no response. I think about telling her what I saw, the letter, but I can't. It could be what Jonesy knew that got her killed.

'Got to go clean it up,' I say and run inside, up to the bathroom, and use toilet paper to clean up the blood.

I'm going to tell the police. I'm going to tell Detective Walker. I'm going to make sure that bastard gets what's coming to him.

53

The next morning I ask Mrs Paterson if it would be all right if I used her phone to call Detective Walker. He told me that if there was anything I could help them with I should call, so that is what I am doing.

Mrs Paterson takes me into her and Mr Paterson's living room. They have their own private space that we are not allowed into. I have only ever been in here once or twice. It smells different to the rest of the house, like stale air that doesn't move around much.

The phone is kept on the windowsill and she takes it down and moves it over to the table so I can dial the number. I haven't used a phone much before so when I try to dial I get it wrong the first two times. Eventually Mrs Paterson takes the number, dials it, checks it is ringing and gives the handset to me. It rings a couple more times, then a female voice says, 'Grant Street Police Station, how can I help you?'

Mrs Paterson stays, which is fine with me as she needs to know what is going on to keep the other girls safe. I ask to speak to Detective Walker and the voice says he isn't at work today, so I tell her that my name is Lesley Beaton, that I live at Cottage 5 at the Homes, and that I want to talk to him, so could he either call the Homes, or if he is going past he could come and visit as I have some important information that could help him.

I'm bursting to tell someone about Mr Sharples. I would talk to Jonesy if she were here. I would talk to Clara if it weren't the school holidays, but I can't trust the girls in my room to keep it to themselves and I don't trust most of the adults around here. They talk to each other so it could get out that way. I want to tell Eadie but it's a Sunday and she's not here. In the end I decide to tell Mrs Paterson. If anything happens to me I need at least one other person to know what I know.

'Mrs Paterson,' I say, 'if the polis call back can you come get me? I think Mr Sharples might be the one killing girls. Please don't tell anyone else yet as I can't prove it, but I found something that might mean it is him.'

She promises to keep quiet about it and I feel a sense of relief to have told someone, although I can tell from her expression that she thinks I'm half cracked.

I go outside to meet up with the girls. I can feel Shona watching me. I know she knows something is up, but she doesn't ask what it is, so I don't tell her.

I'll just wait for Detective Walker to get back to me.

54

The next day I am drying the dishes after tea. They think I'm better now, so I have to join in with the chores again. I don't mind really. I was sick of sitting doing nothing and it was making me feel guilty.

There's a knock at the door, then Pam comes into the kitchen and says there's a man to see me. The girls let out an, 'Oooooohh.' I ignore them, put down the tea towel and go to the front door where Detective Walker is stood waiting for me. I see behind him that his car is parked at the end of our path.

'Hullo, Detective,' I say.

'Hi, Lesley,' he says, 'I got your message, and we were driving home when I suddenly remembered, so ...'

He gestures to the car as he says 'we', so I ask who's in the car.

'Oh that's my fiancée, Lizzie.' He waves at the car and a woman waves back. 'D'you want me to come in, or ...?'

'They'll all listen to us if you come in.'

'We could sit here?'

'They'll listen to us here, too. Chores are just about to finish so they'll be out in a minute. Shall we go for a wee walk?' I suggest.

He looks at the car then back to me. 'Yes, yes that sounds like a good idea, I'll just tell Lizzie.'

'You could tell her where the tearoom is – we could meet her there,' I suggest.

'Yes, yes, another good idea, that's what I'll do.'

He goes to the car window and Lizzie rolls it down and I get a good look at her. She's pretty. She's wearing a light brown cardigan and her hair is dark and tied back.

When he speaks to her she nods and gets out of the car. He gives her some money and points her in the direction of the tearoom.

He watches her walk away, then comes back to me. 'So, how can I help you?' he asks, as we set off walking.

'Lizzie's very pretty. Is she a lot younger than you? Have you been married before?'

'What's this got to do with Morag?'

'Nothing, sorry, she just seems a lot younger than you.'

'Can we stick to why I'm here, please?'

'Aye, sorry. I was thinking, whoever killed Jane and Sally and Jonesy, they have to live here. They have to be on the grounds.'

'And why is that?'

'Because if someone was on the grounds all three times, who's no usually here, it would be obvious because people would want to know whit they were doin'.'

'Good point.'

'So it's someone who's always around. And it's someone who hates women.'

'Why do you say that?'

'Well, why else would you do it if you didnae hate women?'

'I see.'

'So who lives on the grounds and hates women?'

'I don't know.'

'The caretaker.'

I feel bad saying this as Mr Sharples was very nice to me. I feel like I am betraying him but it's more important that we are safe.

'I see, and why do you say that?'

'He's no married, is he? Who's no married at that age? And why is he no married?'

'I don't know.'

'Cos he's ugly. He's ugly and there are all these young girls around and none of them will look at him because he's so hideous and he gets angry and he thinks, *I'll teach them a lesson*. That could be what happened with Jane and Sally.'

'Right …' Detective Walker's gaze is fixed on the trees. 'You think he had a different reason for killing Morag Jones, then?'

'Jonesy was younger than the others. But mibbie she told him how ugly he was, or, or mibbie she worked out it was him whit done it and confronted him, and he saw her behind the cottage and took the opportunity to keep her quiet for good. Think about it. He can go anywhere in the grounds and it wouldn't be suspicious, he's strong enough to have done it.'

I look at Detective Walker to see if he thinks I might be right. I don't think he does, as he grimaces and rubs his cheek.

'I'm sure we interviewed Mr Sharples quite early on, Lesley. But I'll go through the notes.'

'Mibbie he lied?'

'Yes, maybe, maybe.'

'He's got a reason, and he's got the chance to do it. How many people have the reason *and* the chance?'

'Hmmm ...'

I've held back the last bit of information, but Detective Walker still doesn't seem convinced, so I hit him with it. 'And he's a mental.'

'A mental?'

'Aye, he's a lunatic, getting treated at Dykebar, that's where all the lunatics go.'

'And how do you know this?'

'Saw it, didn't I. In his garage, I saw a letter.'

'You've been going through his private property?'

'Had to, sir. They havenae found who did it yet; someone's got to do it.'

'Lesley, I can assure you we have many men investigating this back at the station.'

'Aye, you've got many men, but none of them have found anyone, so mibbie someone else should try. After all, the next person he's gonnae kill isnae going to be one of yous lot, is it? It'll be someone like me, or even me. I cannae just sit about and wait for it to happen, I've got to do something.'

The detective looks at me for a moment. 'It's a good point, Lesley, I can't argue with it, but you shouldn't have done that. There are rules.'

'Aye, but what good are rules if we are all deid?'

'I understand what you are saying, but we have spoken to all the men who live and work at the Homes, they were the first people we looked at, and if there was anything suspicious we would have investigated further.'

'Right …'

'But I'll tell you what,' he says, 'when I'm back at the station tomorrow morning I will read the file on Mr Sharples and see if there is anything in what you have said, a new angle.'

'Angle?'

'Yes, you know, a different way of looking at it.'

'Why is that an angle?'

'Well, Lesley, when you have a problem like the one we have here it pays to look at things from a number of different positions, or angles, to see if it looks different when viewed from another place. See that bush over there?'

'Aye.'

'Well that bush will look different to us when we're standing here to if we were over there,' he said, pointing at the junction, 'and it's the same with a problem or a case.'

'I see. All right. Thank you, sir.'

'And I'll come back and let you know what I find.'

Our walk is now leading us towards the tearoom.

'Detective Walker,' I say.

'Yes?'

'Why did you no get engaged until now?'

'I guess I hadn't met the right woman.'

'And is Lizzie the right woman?

'I think so, yes.'

'She's very pretty.'

'I think she is, yes.'

'Does she like going out with a policeman?'

'I hope so.'

'Are you having a baby, sir?'

'I'm sorry?'

'Are you havin' a baby, is that why you're getting married?'

'Why do you say that?'

'Because that's why a lot of people get married. And she touched her stomach when she got out of the car.'

'You are a perceptive girl, Lesley, if a nosey one. You will make a fine detective one day, I think.'

'Oh, I don't want to be a detective; I want to be a scientist.'

'Well, good for you, Lesley, good for you. You'll need to study hard to be one of those.'

'I will, sir, and congratulations.'

'I think it's time you went back, don't you?'

'Are you going to walk me back?'

'Err ...'

'There's a dangerous man on the loose.'

'All right, then yes, and I'll pick up the car.'

He walks me back to Cottage 5 and I ask him how long he has been a detective and if he likes it. His answers are: three years, after being a normal policeman for two years; and yes, he does like it. But he says sometimes it isn't very nice, you see some very unpleasant things, and sometimes have to give people very bad news.

When we get to his car I say goodbye and walk up to the cottage. I sit on the step to watch him drive off to pick up Lizzie from the tearoom.

I don't tell the girls what I have told Detective Walker; if they know they might let it slip and Mr Sharples would find out. But I start to worry that I don't want them to go anywhere near him or his hut, so when the lights go out and we're all lying in bed, I tell them I think Mr Sharples is creepy, and I'm not going to go anywhere near him until they have caught the murderer. That way I haven't accused him of doing anything, but I have said enough so the girls will keep an eye out for him.

I go to sleep thinking about Lizzie. I wonder if she will get into trouble for being pregnant and not being married. I'm never going to get pregnant without being married; that's how I ended up here in the first place.

55

I wake up early next morning. I seem to be waking up early a lot and failing to get back to sleep. My first thought is often, *Is Jonesy in her bed?* Then I remember she won't be, then I can't get back to sleep. Sometimes I'm awake for hours before the others get up. I just lie there staring at the ceiling, or I turn to stare out of the window. I'm staring but I'm not seeing, my eyes are looking but not focusing.

Mrs Paterson stops me as I'm leaving the cottage with Shona. 'Lesley, can you wait a minute?' she says. 'Shona, you go on without her; this is going to take a bit of time.'

When she says that, I feel sick. I immediately try to think of what I've done wrong. She and Mr Paterson have been so nice to me since Jonesy died that I've forgotten what it's like to be told off. Maybe now I'm going to find out.

'Can you go and wait for me in our living room?' she says.

I go into their living room, back with its smell and the phone I used before to call Detective Walker. I wait there for about ten minutes trying to work out what I'm in here for when the door opens. A woman comes in, followed by Mrs Paterson.

I stand up and try to work out who she is. She's thin – ill-thin – her eyes are sunken and her hair is thin, too, like an old person's. But she isn't old and her hair isn't grey; she's probably about thirty and her hair is a reddish brown. Her clothes are well worn, as if they were smart once, but over time have lost any hint of smartness.

'Lesley, this is someone who would like to meet you,' says Mrs Paterson, motioning to the lady. 'This is Margaret Jones. She's Morag Jones's mother, and she's asked if it would be all right to chat to you.'

I look at Jonesy's mum, and she looks at me.

Mrs Paterson says, 'I thought you would like to meet her; is that all right?'

I nod. I try to remember everything Jonesy ever told me about her mum, why Jonesy was put in here, why she hardly ever saw her. Her mother didn't even come to the funeral.

The woman comes over and holds my hands and looks deep into my eyes. 'I can see why Morag would have been good friends with you. You're a wee doll, aren't you?' she says, smiling and shaking a little.

'Take a seat on the sofa, you two, and I'll fetch you some tea.'

She lets go of my hands and we sit down at the same time. Mrs Paterson backs away out of the room.

Jonesy's mum picks up my hands again.

'You Lesley?' she says gently.

I nod.

'That's a bonnie name. My name is Margaret, everyone calls me Mags, expect Morag may have told you, aye?'

I nod. She hadn't. She had never mentioned her name.

The woman is speaking very softly and her hands start to feel shaky.

'D'you like it here?'

I nod.

'How old are you?'

'Twelve.'

'Aye,' she says, 'same age as Morag, heh?'

We both sit in silence after she says that. I don't know what to say to her. I don't know if it would be betraying Jonesy if I am nice to her. I don't think Jonesy liked her. I can't ever remember her visiting. Margaret Jones holds onto my hands and looks round the room.

Eventually the silence is ended when Mrs Paterson comes back in with a tray carrying a teapot and two cups.

When I see it is only two cups I realise Mrs Paterson isn't going to stay and I am going to have to talk some more to Jonesy's mum on my own.

'How are you two getting along?' says a smiling Mrs Paterson.

'Fine,' I say.

'I'll just pour you both a cup and leave you alone.' Mrs Paterson pours the tea into the pale blue cups and pushes the milk jug towards us. 'I'll be in the kitchen if you need me.'

When she leaves there is another silence, then Margaret speaks. 'Must have been hard for you?'

'It was. It still is.'

'How long were you two best pals?'

'For ever. We were always best friends.'

'And you shared a room?'

I nod. 'Same room,' I say, 'sometimes same bed.'

'Could you tell me about her?'

'Sure,' I say.

'The thing is, I didnae get to know her like you got to know her. They took her away from me. Said I was a bad mother, said I wasnae capable of looking after her. I *was* capable. I loved her. I'd have done anything for her, but they took her from me. Said I couldnae take care of myself. That's when I started with the drink.

'Always liked a drink, me, but see, when Morag came along I was good, I was real good. Me and her da didnae last too long. He wasnae a good man, so it was probably for the best, but see when they see a woman on her own with a baby, they're looking for a reason to take it aff you.

'Once they took her away I couldnae cope. Not with the one thing I loved gone. That's when I struggled. And when they see you struggling, well, they're never going to bring her back then.'

I can see the pain in her. Her hands are shaking even more as she speaks.

'When I heard what had happened to Morag, that was me gone. I couldnae continue. I heard the news and next thing I know it's days later. I couldnae tell you what happened in between. Woke up in the hospital. Said they'd found me in Dundee. I don't know anyone in Dundee. Never have.

'Och, listen to me going on, I shouldnae talk about

me. I want to talk to you, you were gonnae tell me about Morag.'

She's wiping her tears away. I think of what she's said, of what she wants to hear. What would make her feel better?

'I don't know where to start.'

'Was she funny?'

'Oooh, was she? She was crazy. She was always doing daft stuff to make us all laugh. She was never happier than when she'd made us crease up with laughter.'

'That's nice. When I pictured her, I always pictured her with friends.'

'Aye, she would be with friends. She had friends at the school and at our cottage. She was a bit of a one. She wasn't like the others.'

'She was special?'

'Oh yes, she was special, all right. There wasnae another one like her. She was so full of energy.'

'I imagine you miss her very much.'

I start to cry too. I can't help it. I am just about to say that it feels like I am missing my arm, something that has always been there and now is suddenly not there, but I can't say it, I can't say anything.

'Och, I'm sorry, doll. That was a stupid thing for me to say, a stupid thing. Of course you miss her. I miss her and I never got to spend any time with her. I remember my best friend when I was your age. Bertha Campbell, thick as thieves we were. Went everywhere together. Such good friends. She moved away before we were teenagers. Never saw her again.'

I'm still crying, but a bit less. 'Sorry,' I say. 'When I talk about Jonesy it just makes me so sad ... I always end up ... it's why I stopped talking about her ... but then when you stop it ... next time ... just comes out.'

'Oh I know, I know, I'm sorry, doll, I just wanted to get close to her in some way. Now she's gone you're the closest thing I've got to her.'

I nod.

'When Morag was born I'd never been happier. When I first held her I swore that day I would change. I knew I hadnae been the best behaved person before, but as soon as I looked into her eyes I knew I had to change, and I did. I got myself straight. She was a very wee baby, just over four pounds, but she was a fighter, and I was gonnae fight to give her the best life I could.

'And I tried, I tried so hard. I brought her home and Billy, her dad, he didnae know how to cope. When I'd got pregnant it hadn't been intentional, but he'd seemed happy, talked about mibbie one day marrying me. But he wasnae a nice man, Morag's dad, he didnae treat me well. And there's me looking after her while he was going out and cavorting. It was embarrassing. I was hearing what he had been getting up to, and then he was coming home after a drink and he was bad, real bad.

'I had to leave him, It wasnae safe for either me or Morag. We moved back to Hamilton, but I had no family I could stay with. It was no good. We were in this one-bedroom place, just me and her against the world. But Billy went spare. When he found out we'd gone he smashed the place to pieces.

'Anyways, one day the polis knock on the door, says we are in danger. Says they've heard he knows where I am, says he's coming for us both. I said, cannae they arrest him, and they said he's not done anything wrong. We moved to Aberdeen for six weeks. When we were up there the polis called and told me that Billy's dead. Got drunk, got angry, got in a fight, got killed. No witnesses but they think it was more than one person whit done it.

'I felt so relieved. You should never wish anyone dead, Lesley, but this is a man who won't be missed. Such a shame that he was the one who was Morag's dad.

'So I moved back to Hamilton and we're back in the one-bed flat. But Billy's mum starts putting round all these stories that I cannae look after the bairn on my own, and that it wisnae safe for Morag. I mean, that's her own granddaughter she's talking about. They took Morag away from me. Said she'd be better looked after if she was in care. I cannae tell you what that feels like, Lesley. There's no words for when somebody does that to you.'

She starts to cry.

'Oh, look at me. I'm sorry, doll.'

Mrs Paterson knocks, then comes in. 'You two all right in here?'

I nod.

Mags turns to me. 'Will you write to me?'

'Of course.'

She writes down her address, then stands up. I get up too and she gives me a hug; I can hear her sniffing as she does.

Mrs Paterson sees her to the front door. When she comes back she asks me how it was. I tell her it was nice to meet her but that she was a bit strange. She asks if I want to go to Jonesy's grave in Paisley later that day and I say yes.

*

After dinner Mrs Paterson drives me to the cemetery. I didn't know she could drive too, as it's always Mr Paterson who does the driving. We picked some flowers from the garden, so when we get to her grave we lay them down.

Mrs Paterson says she's off to find a shop to get some bread, so I sit down next to the grave so I can talk to Jonesy. There is no headstone yet. Apparently it's coming soon.

'Hiya, Jonesy,' I say, 'how you doing down there? Or is it up there? I dinnae know if you are lying under all this or up in heaven.

'We've kept your bed in the room. I still havenae given up hope that you might come back to use it. The whole room misses you, it's just not the same any more. Shona talks even more now you've gone. I like her but I wish she'd shut it sometimes.

'Your mammy came to see me. She misses you even though she never came to see you. Sounds like your real dad was a bastard so you might have been lucky to not have been with them. She's awfy thin. Thinnest person I've ever seen. She looks like you could see right through her.

'School's been good, people were being nicer to me when we broke up. Remember when I said they didnae speak to me much and left me on my own? They talk to me now, and I've got friends there. No friends like you, though, no proper friends, just school friends.

'I'm gonnae get the bastard who did this to you, Jonesy, I'm going to get them so bad and when they go to hang them I'm going to pull that bloody lever and watch them choke.

'Dinnae tell anyone I said that.

'I think I know who might have done it; I think it might have been Mr Sharples, the caretaker. You cannae tell me, can you? Can you give me a sign? I told Detective Walker. I like him. He's got a girlfriend and he's got her pregnant and now he's got to marry her. I said Sharples was a weirdy and, get this, he's a nutter too, saw a letter in his garage. And he's ugly, which is why he probably hates women.'

I hear Mrs Paterson walking up behind me. 'Got to go now, Jonesy. I'll come back to see you, don't worry, I won't leave you here alone. I hope you've made friends – knowing you, you will have. I hope you are stirring up the dead oldies down there. I'll be back, never fear, keep you in nice flowers. Bye, Jonesy. Bye, my pal.'

Mrs Paterson and I drive back to the Homes in silence.

It feels good to have had the chance to have a chat with Jonesy.

I hope she heard me.

56

Eadie comes to the cottage to get me the next afternoon. I'm wearing my best clothes. I haven't been able to concentrate all day for thinking about meeting the couple who might want to adopt me.

Eadie walks with me up to the tearoom. She tells me their names are Mr and Mrs Anderson. He is a doctor and she helps out at a school. Eadie says that because they are smart people, and I am bright, we will be a really good match. She says they will be able to help me with my schooling. Imagine being able to come home and speak to someone who could actually help me learn more.

I can feel my nerves as I walk. I think I am breathing too much. I tell Eadie I'm scared. She says they are good and kind people, and that I am a nice person, so I should just be myself – but what if they don't like the myself that I am? Plenty of people here don't like me.

When we get to the tearoom I can see a couple sat by a table at the far wall and I know it is them; they look so different to the type of people who are usually in the tearoom, they are neatly dressed, and I know this is a strange thing to think, but they look clever.

He has a long blue coat on, a black briefcase by his side, and brown hair which has faded back across most of his head. He has a moustache and glasses that make him look a little like a professor. What there is of his hair is curly and tight. She is wearing a patterned skirt with a cardigan on top. She has glasses, too, but hers are a fun shade of yellow.

As Eadie opens the door I suddenly pull back.

'What's the matter?' she asks.

'I cannae do it.'

'Sure you can, there's nothing to it.'

'What if they don't like me?' I say, shaking now.

'Lesley, there's nothing not to like.'

'There's lots of things not to like.'

'I'm sure they don't, and if they do, maybe they're just jealous.'

'They're no.'

'They are. But you're just looking at this from your point of view, Lesley. The Andersons are going to be nervous too, they're going to hope that *you* like *them*. Unless you like them, they have no chance of you staying with them, so think of it like that. Nothing happens unless you decide it does.'

I look away for a moment, across to the main road that leads towards the entrance gate. Some boys are running around holding sticks, no doubt off to break something. I turn back to Eadie, breathe out slowly and say, 'All right, I'm ready.'

We walk across the room and I see some of the house-fathers having a break from their cottages. One of them is Mr Roberts, the housefather of Cottage 14 who batters the boys, and I remember why I want to get out of here so much.

Mrs Anderson sees Eadie first and nudges her husband and they both get up and turn to face us.

'Eadie, so good to see you,' says Mrs Anderson. Her accent isn't Glaswegian, it's softer than from round here, a bit English, like they sound on the radio. I decide to make mine more proper.

'And you must be Lesley,' she says, smiling and offering her hand.

I lean forward to shake it and curtsey. I don't know why I curtsey, it's such a stupid thing to do. *You idiot, Lesley.* My face starts to heat up with embarrassment.

'We've heard so much about you, Lesley,' says Mrs Anderson, 'but Eadie didn't tell us how pretty you are.'

People never say I am pretty. I'm not ugly but people never talk about me as being one of the pretty ones. I think she is just saying it to be nice to me, but I don't mind, it's nice of her to say it.

'Hello there,' her husband says as he leans around Eadie and offers a hand too. He smiles at me and I can smell coffee on his breath.

'Hello, Mr Anderson,' I say.

'Actually, it's Dr Anderson – did Eadie mention I was a doctor?'

'Yes, sorry, Dr Anderson.'

'There's no need to be sorry, Lesley. Would you like to see my doctor kit?'

I nod and he gets out his listening device from his briefcase.

'This is a stethoscope,' he says. 'Would you like to try it?'

I nod again.

'You can use this to listen to everything that's going on in your body. Do you want to listen to your own heartbeat?'

I nod.

He attaches the listening bits to my ears and says, 'Right, put this bit where you think your heart is.'

I put it in the middle of my chest.

'Very good,' he says, 'but it's a little bit over to the left,' and points to the strap on my dress. 'Now try.'

I can hear it. My heart is going bi-dum ... bi-dum ... bi-dum.

'Can you hear two beats each time?' he asks. 'That's because there are two beats to every heartbeat. Did you know that?'

I shake my head.

'Because every time it beats there's a mini-beat first, so one half, the smaller half of the heart, beats first, then the bigger part beats, and that's the big beat.' He drums out the pattern on the table, with one hand doing a little tap, followed quickly by the other doing a big tap.

'Gerald,' says Mrs Anderson, 'she doesn't need a medical lecture.' She turns to me. 'Now, Lesley, can I get you and Eadie something to drink?'

'A cup of tea, please.'

'A cup of tea?' she says. 'How very grown-up.'

I smile.

We sit and chat for half an hour. They are definitely intelligent people, like Eadie.

*

Eventually I have to go back to the cottage for tea, but before I leave Mrs Anderson asks me if I would like to come to their house and spend the weekend with them. She says they have a dog and a cat they would like me to meet. They live in Airdrie on the other side of Glasgow. I tell them I would like to go very much.

As I leave Mrs Anderson waves me off and Dr Anderson smiles again. Eadie tells them she will take me back to Cottage 5, then come back for them. I say there's no need, I can make my own way back.

As I walk I am really smiling. I feel happy, I feel excited. I haven't felt happy or excited since before Jonesy died. I feel bad for feeling happy, but I can't help it. The Andersons seemed really nice and they seemed to like me. This could be my way out of this place; I could have a family and live in a proper home like a normal girl, in a normal house, with normal parents.

I could have my own bedroom to sleep in. That would be unbelievable. I wouldn't have Jonesy back, but I would have something for me, finally.

57

I'm on my way back from a walk around the fields when I see Shona sitting on the steps of Cottage 5. She spots me and comes racing over.

'You were right, you were right, you were right!' she says, almost out of breath.

'Right about what?'

'Two polis cars turned up; they went to see Sharples. They're with him now. Shall we go and looky?'

'Naw,' I say, then, 'Aye.'

I knew it, I think, *I knew he was odd and I knew I was right to say something.* I feel excited and relieved, but I don't tell Shona that it was me that told on him.

As we walk across the road to the farmhouse there's a big crowd of children standing about trying to get a look at what's going on. We try to get to the front but there's a policeman telling everyone, in very rude words, that we should go away now.

No one moves.

Then he says he will give us ten seconds, then he will

call the Superintendent and if any of us are still here when Mr Gordon arrives, we will be punished.

That works and we all move away.

Shona and I walk back towards our cottage. We see Mary at the bridge over the stream so go and let her know what's happening. We sit on the bridge and wait. After about twenty minutes we see a police car leaving. As it goes past, we can see Mr Sharples sat in the back. His head is bowed down so we can't see his eyes but it is definitely him; he must be so ashamed of what he's done. There's a blue car behind the police car, which I recognise as Detective Walker's.

I get down off the wall and wave at him. He stops and winds down the window.

'I told you, I told you!' I say. 'Did you arrest him?'

'Lesley, I can't talk about this.'

'But I was right, wasn't I? It was him! I was right.'

'Lesley, what did I just say?'

'Sorry, sir.'

'Now please do not discuss this with anyone, understand?'

'Aye,' I say, but even as I say it, I know I am lying.

It is all we talk about that afternoon, it is all we talk about at tea, and all we talk about in our room. I finally tell the girls that I was the one who tipped the police off. They say they had thought it was him all along, too, but I know they didn't.

I go to bed feeling safe for the first time in a long time. I can't believe they let him live here all this time after he'd done it and he could have killed more girls. I think of the time I walked Petal with him; maybe he was thinking of killing me then, and when he said Petal could keep secrets maybe he told Petal what he had done to Jane and Sally. Then I think of what he did to Jonesy and I think how I hope they kill him now.

58

On Saturday morning I keep waking up to see if it is time to get up yet. I lie in my bed waiting for the sun to rise. Shona comes over to see how I am. With Morag gone, Shona is the girl in my room I talk to most, despite our disagreements before. She is excited for me.

I'm so nervous. I've borrowed one of Mrs Paterson's suitcases to pack my things for staying at the Andersons', and packed and unpacked it three times. I've never been out of the Homes for a weekend on my own. Some children get to spend the occasional weekend with relatives or parents, but my mum isn't one for that; she will only see me here. Gran talks about having me to stay but I think Mum is against it. I would like to have stayed with Gran.

Shona and I go down to breakfast, and after doing the tidying chores I run back upstairs to make sure I've packed everything again.

Eadie comes to the cottage to check on me. She doesn't live at the Homes and usually she doesn't work weekends in the summer holidays so it is kind of her to come to see me off. She says she was just passing so thought it would be nice to pop in, but I know she wouldn't have been passing.

Dr and Mrs Anderson arrive at Cottage 5 just after half past nine. They pull up in a dark blue car that looks new and spotlessly clean. They get out of the car and Eadie walks me over to them and starts chatting.

'Let me help you with that,' says Dr Anderson, as he takes the suitcase. When he feels its weight he says, 'You planning on staying a couple of months, then?'

I laugh nervously. I just wanted to make sure I had everything in case I needed to change clothes.

As we drive off, I wave goodbye to Mrs Paterson and Shona. The seats in the back of the car look like white leather. I sit in the middle and Mrs Anderson – she insists I call her Anne, but I'm always forgetting – keeps turning round to ask me questions. Dr Anderson – Gerald – watches the road while he drives, occasionally chipping in with a comment.

Mrs Anderson asks me a lot about school, what I like, what I don't like. She asks how it was being the only person in my year at the Homes to go to the grammar school. I try to sound positive.

At some point I must have fallen asleep as next thing I see is their house. They have a bungalow, up a steep drive. Dr Anderson pulls the brake sharply to make sure the car won't roll back down, then we all get out.

I can hear their dog barking right away. Mrs Anderson sees that I look scared and tells me not to worry. 'He's very friendly,' she says.

'I'm not sure dogs like me.'

'Oh this one will, he's a big softy. You wait till you meet him. His name is Bertie.'

She opens the front door and Bertie comes rushing out. The cat flies out of the house at the same time, as if it is delighted to escape being locked inside with a crazy dog.

Bertie goes straight up to Mrs Anderson and rears on his back legs, pawing at her hips. He then rushes round the other side of the car to Dr Anderson, who tells him to get down.

Then he sees me, and comes up and starts sniffing me.

'He isn't angry, just interested,' says Dr Anderson.

Mrs Anderson says, 'Come away, Bertie!' and pulls at his collar. Bertie fights against her at first, but then does as he's told.

'This is our home, Lesley,' says Mrs Anderson. 'If at any time you want to go back, just let me know and we can drive you straight back to the cottage. We want you to enjoy your weekend with us, but we realise you don't know us that well and this could all seem a little strange. Right, let me show you to your room.'

The house seems odd. There's a smell as soon as you come in, like the forest smell out the back of the Homes. It hits me the minute I'm through the door. Also there are things on every flat surface in the hall. There are little model dogs on a shelf, a cartoon drawing of a golfer on the windowsill, and photographs lined up on a cabinet. Everything has something on it.

The room I am staying in is their 'guest room'; it has

a double bed. I've never slept in one before and the first thing I think is, *They won't believe me when I get back.*

'Gerald will bring your suitcase in from the car. In the meantime, I'll just let you get used to your room. There's a bathroom across the hall, and the kitchen and living room are down there. But I'll give you the full tour later.'

Mrs Anderson leaves the room and I have a chance to look around. The window looks out to the neighbour's house. The wallpaper is a pale green, with thin light lines going down it. There are more things on the chest of drawers – little cat statuettes, this time.

After a while the door nudges open and in comes the cat that escaped earlier. It walks straight into the room and jumps on the bed, then looks at me as if to tell me, *This is my bed, and don't you think of taking it.*

I hold out my hand and after a moment of thought it rubs its head and neck up against it.

'Hello yoooouuu,' I say. 'What's your name?' It's funny cos I am talking in my posh accent to the Andersons but I'm talking in my even posher voice to the cat in case it tells them that I'm no good.

It purrs and keeps rubbing up against my arm. I sit on the bed and it lets me stroke it. The cat and I have a good chat and it eventually walks onto my lap where it pads its feet. I think we have come to an understanding, and I will be allowed to stay in the room and sleep in the bed after all.

Mrs Anderson comes back, and says, 'So I see you've met Mog.'

'Yes, I think we've become friends.'

'That's strange. Mog doesn't take to people too easily; she must really like you.'

I smile at that.

'Now, what would you like to do this weekend? We could take a drive to the coast, we could go for a walk, or we could drive into Glasgow.'

'Ooh, Glasgow, Glasgow, please!' I say. I've never been there before and the chances to go to a city are so rare.

'Righty-o,' she says. 'If we're going to Glasgow we should head off now so we can get there for dinner.' She walks out to tell Dr Anderson that we're going to drive into town. I hear some discussion about whether he wants to go too, but when they come out of the kitchen they seem happy and so we set off.

There is a lot less talking on the way to Glasgow. I am so excited at the chance to go to shops and see the sights. When we arrive, Dr Anderson parks the car and Mrs Anderson finds a café she has eaten in before and they say they will just squeeze us in before the kitchen closes.

Mrs Anderson asks what I want from the menu and I don't know what to get so I say I'll eat whatever she's having, which is an omelette. Dr Anderson says he will have the same 'to keep it simple', then Mrs Anderson buys me a cola and we sit in a booth.

'Anything you want to see?' asks Mrs Anderson.

'Shops,' I say. 'Shops and maybe some more shops.'

Dr Anderson laughs and shakes his head.

'What sort of shops?' asks Mrs Anderson.

'Oh, clothes shops, please.'

'I'll see what I can do.'

The omelettes come and we scoff them down, Dr Anderson pays and we go walking down Sauchiehall Street. There are shops as far as you can see. Dr Anderson looks bored, but Mrs Anderson is as excited as me. It's so busy. There's more people than I've ever seen in my life.

'All right, Lesley,' Mrs Anderson says, 'this is a one-off, but we are going to buy you something as this is a special treat.'

I want to hug her but I don't as I think she might find it strange. I think of how incredibly jealous the girls will be when I come back with something new.

We walk the entire length of Sauchiehall Street, going into the shops and inspecting all the different clothes. By the end I can see Dr Anderson wants to go home. He peers into a shop window with a big crowd of people in front of it, to see the football scores. Once he's seen them, he announces it is time to go. I haven't chosen anything yet, so we go back to the first shop and I choose a black skirt, and Mrs Anderson buys herself a scarf.

I want to write down everything that has happened so I don't forget it. I have to tell Shona and the girls everything.

59

The drive back goes quickly. I try to take in everything I see as I know I won't see it again for a long time. Who knows, though, if I come to live with the Andersons maybe I'll go to Glasgow all the time.

When we arrive at the house I can see Bertie the dog at the door already; he must be able to sense when the car is coming back. As soon as Mrs Anderson opens the door he rushes out down the drive, then to Mrs Anderson, then to Dr Anderson, then to sniff me. I am still not sure around him, he's just a bit over-excited.

Mrs Anderson says I should go to my room and try the skirt on while she starts tea, then if I want I can come and help her.

I try it on and look at myself in the mirror. I love it. I am going to keep it hidden in my room for a week before I show the girls, then just wear it casually next weekend as if it were nothing. They won't know where I got it.

Mrs Anderson is making mince an' tatties in the kitchen. The mince is already on the hob and I help peel the potatoes. Dr Anderson sits in the garden reading his newspaper with a bottle of beer. When tea's ready we call him in and we all sit round the table.

They don't say grace. Every meal I have ever had at the Homes someone says grace. I almost ask them why, then I think maybe they don't believe in God either. I won't ask this time as it might be considered rude, but I am definitely going to ask them eventually.

The mince an' tatties are amazing. Cook makes it all the time but never like this, it just tastes so, so good. The Andersons ask me about the trouble at the Homes, but I just say I don't know much about it. Mrs Anderson says that after tea they like to have some quiet time listening to the radio, then maybe a quick game of cards, then I can go to bed.

We all sit in the living room and listen to the BBC on the wireless. Dr Anderson gets out his cigarettes and smokes two. Mrs Anderson explains how he likes to have a couple after his tea but rarely smokes at any other time.

After he's smoked the second cigarette, and the fog has disappeared, we get out the cards. The game is called Knock-out Whist. Mrs Anderson teaches me the rules and I love it. What a clever game. I lose the first one but win the next two. I think they may have let me win but it is great fun.

Eventually Dr Anderson declares I am too good and I will need to go to bed before his feelings are hurt. Mrs Anderson tucks me in and, after she's gone, I try so hard not to think it, I do everything I can to distract myself, but I can't help it, the thought just keeps coming back – one day, this could be my home.

Mog jumps up on the bed and curls up near my middle. This might have been my best day ever.

*

I wake up full of hope, which I haven't felt in so long.

After breakfast we don't have to go to church. No grace and no church is such a joy.

Dr Anderson gives me some of the newspaper to read, but after that it's time to pack and get back in the car. I say goodbye to Mog and make a mental promise that I will see her again.

We get back around noon, just before dinner. The Homes look somewhat greyer than before I left. It's a sunny day but the buildings don't reflect it. I don't mind, though, as this is not going to be my home for much longer.

I am excited about telling the girls everything that has happened. I find them round the back of the cottage. They stop what they're doing and rush over, asking loads of questions and I tell them what it was like and how nice the Andersons were. They seem excited for me; I am excited for me. I am trying not to be too excited, but I can't help myself.

60

The next day we are out of milk at the cottage. 'Go and get us some from the shop,' says Cook, giving me the money.

'Want to come with me, Eldrey?' I say. 'I'm off out to get some milk.'

'Nuh,' she says.

I think a month ago she would have come with me. A week ago I would have had three of them with me. They must think I'm back to normal now. I'm not, but there's only so long they can be that nice to me. And the adults seem to have stopped making us go everywhere in pairs. They used to shout at us if they saw us on our own, but now they seem to have given up.

I walk along Faith Avenue and I see a black car coming towards me. It's flash, very shiny. I stop to look; so do other children. We don't get too many cars down these roads and we definitely don't get cars as nice as this.

I look to see who's driving, but they have a hat on and I can't quite see the face. I watch it go past then turn back and cross into Church Road.

As I do I suddenly spot Mr Sharples in front of me. He's carrying a large sack on his shoulder. He's seen me, and he's seen me watching the car.

I take a short breath.

'Hey, you,' he says.

I try to look away.

'No, you, I wanna word wi' you.'

I feel scared. He puts the sack down and walks towards me. 'You're the one that's been talking to the polis, right?'

I look at the ground.

'You think I had somethin' to do with those deid girls, right?'

I look up at him this time and nod, then back down again.

'You think I'm a weirdy, don't you? Think I'm a bit strange?'

I don't respond to this.

'Look at me.'

I look up again.

'Aye, so you do. I might be a bit different, and I'm no so good with people, but I didnae have nothing to do with them lassies, see?'

I nod vigorously.

'So dinnae go tellin' people that I did, cos I didnae.'

I nod again.

'On you go.'

A cold pulse goes down my back. I know I'm supposed to go get milk but instead I just turn round and run back to the cottage. I go straight to my bedroom and dive onto my bed.

Eldrey is in there with Shona.

'Whit is it?' she asks.

'Nuthin'.'

'You sure?'

'Aye.'

They leave the room.

Five minutes later, Cook comes in.

'Where's my milk?' she says.

'They ran out.'

'Ran out, eh? Could you no have told us, no?'

'Sorry.'

And I *am* sorry. I shouldn't have said anything to the police, I had no proof. I need proof.

61

I go to see Eadie. One other person is waiting to see her and it's Glenda McAdam.

When I see her and she looks at me I think I might be for it, but she says, 'Hullo,' so I say, 'Hullo,' back.

There is silence for a minute. I look at the wall. I can feel her staring at me but I am not going to stare back. Eventually she breaks the silence and says, 'Whit you here for?'

I don't know what to say. I try to think of a lie but it doesn't come quick enough, so I just tell the truth. 'There's a couple who want to adopt me, I think.'

'That's nice,' she says. 'D'you wanna go?'

'I dunno. Think so, think it would be nice.'

'You should definitely go; you'd suit a normal family. Some of us are best aff here, but it would be good for you.'

I feel odd. She's being friendly. I've never seen her be nice, but then I have never seen her not surrounded by her scraggy friends.

'Whit are you here for?' I ask.

'Da's gone psycho again. He's attacked a policeman and gone missing. They're worried he's going to turn up here. Eadie asked to see me; she's worried about me.'

'Have you seen her before?'

'Oh, aye, come here all the time.'

'Really?'

For some reason her saying this makes me feel betrayed. I know Eadie sees lots of other kids, but I didn't know Glenda was one of them. She'd never said.

'Oh, aye, for the last couple of years. They worry about me cos of my family. Used to hate coming but now I kinda like it. It's a chance to get away from everyone.'

'She's good, isn't she?' I say.

'I dunno if she's good, I just know it's nice that someone listens to me.'

The door to the office opens. A scruffy boy of about eight or nine comes sprinting out. Glenda looks at me and says, 'Well, I'll see you later.'

'All right,' I reply and give a little wave.

Eadie puts her head round the door. 'Hi Lesley,' she says. 'You happy to wait?'

I nod.

'Good, get yourself a book. I'm sure I won't be too long,' and she shuts the door.

I don't get a book. I stare at the wall instead and try to work out if Glenda being there counts as a betrayal. It shouldn't, Eadie shouldn't have favourites, but still I thought she really liked me. She probably *does* like me; it doesn't mean she doesn't like other people. She could like Glenda, and Glenda is not very likeable, but then Glenda was nice earlier and maybe she's only horrible because she's from a bad family and maybe she's not bad herself, maybe that family just makes you bad, so it's not her fault.

I can't stop my thoughts going around.

After a long time the door opens again and Glenda leaves. She says goodbye to me as she goes.

It must be strange for Eadie; people go into her room feeling one way and come out feeling another. She's like a hairdresser for people's emotions.

I go into the room and sit in the chair. It still feels warm from Glenda's bottom. I've never said anything about Glenda or the fight to Eadie. Perhaps she already knows. Glenda might have said something, back when it happened.

'How are we, Lesley?'

'Good, I think.'

'And how were the Andersons?'

'Good, it was good, they were good. Yeah, really good.'

'So do you think you might want to live with them?'

'Yeah, I think, yeah, I think I would.'

'You need to really think about this, Lesley, because this is a big decision. You would be leaving here, and your cottage, and your friends, and although you won't never see them again, you certainly wouldn't see them very much. If you leave you would really leave.'

'I know,' I say. 'I have been thinking about it a lot. If Jonesy was still here it would be hard and I think I would say no, but she's not, and it's not the same any more. The cottage did feel like home, but now it feels like a place where I sleep and eat in between school.'

Eadie looks at me for a while. 'All right,' she says finally, 'here's what I want you to do: think about it for two more days, and if it's still a yes, either pop in to see me or write me a letter.'

I nod in agreement, but I know what my answer will be. I want to go live with the Andersons.

*

I am as good as my word. Two days later I go to see Eadie and tell her I have thought about it some more and that I definitely want to live with the Andersons.

She tells me that is great news and that she thinks I will be very happy.

The one thing that had been bothering me is that I won't get to see her any more, but she answers that question before I even ask, saying she will make sure she comes to see me once a fortnight either at the Andersons' house or at my school.

I feel relieved.

She says she will put the wheels in motion.

I feel happy but nervous and I decide to tell the other girls in my room. Shona asks if they want to take two girls instead of just one.

I think they are happy for me. Sometimes I think no one wants anyone else to do well or escape as it just makes those left behind feel bad. I can't think like that. I need to do this for me.

62

Shona and I are walking to the shop to get sweeties. Shona's mum gave her two shillings on her last visit. She didn't tell anyone but last night when everyone went to sleep she told me, and said that after breakfast we'd go and get a bag of sweets.

We're coming past the main road when I see Detective Walker getting out of his car. He sees me and looks down as if he hasn't. I tell Shona I'm sorry but I have to go.

'Mr Walker! Mr Walker!' I shout. He is still looking down, so I don't think he hears me. I run after him. When I catch up with him, he looks surprised.

'Mr Walker,' I say, 'is there any news? Do you have a new suspect?'

'It's *Detective* Walker, Lesley, and there's no more news at the moment. I was just going to see the Superintendent to give him an update.'

'So ... it wasnae Mr Sharples?'

'No, Lesley, it wasn't. He can account for his whereabouts for all the times of the attacks and there are people who can verify those claims, so we have ruled him out for the time being.'

'I'm sorry, I just thought—'

'Thank you for trying to help us, but you shouldn't judge people just because they are a bit different.'

'Sorry.'

'Like I said, thanks for your help, though.'

'Well, is there anyone else? Because they are still out there and people seem to have forgotten about that. People here are carrying on as if everything is normal and it's no. There's still a killer about.'

'Yes, Lesley, believe me, we haven't forgotten.'

'So you have other suspects? Who are they?'

'We have some people of interest, but I would be seriously undermining the investigation if I were to tell you who they were.'

'Oh ... all right.'

'Now, if you'll excuse me, I'd like to get in to see Mr Gordon. Thank you.' He smiles at me but he doesn't mean it.

I watch him go inside the executive building where the Super's office is, and think about waiting for him to come back out. I could help the police, I am the person who is here all the time, I am the one who sees what's going on. I was closest to Jonesy. I have to be of some use to them.

I stand in the same spot for the next five minutes, unsure of what I should do next, when I remember Shona and the sweet shop. When I get to the shop she's just leaving. I catch up with her but she says I can't have any sweets as I didn't come with her to buy them. I tell her I had to talk to the policeman, but it doesn't seem to matter to her.

She tries to walk a little faster and leave me behind, but I keep up with her, so she tries to walk faster still. In the end we are almost running back to the house.

I stop and let her get away. If she wants to be silly, she can; there are more important things than sweets.

'Suit yerself,' I say as she goes.

She doesn't speak to me for the next two days.

63

A week later I still haven't heard anything about the Andersons, so I go to see Eadie to find out what the news is.

As I arrive at the hospital building, I see a boy coming out with his face wrapped in bandages. You can see dried blood on his nose. It looks like he's had a 'doing'. If it isn't the houseparents it's the boys themselves 'doing' each other. For the boys there seems to be nothing more exciting than a fight. First the hope of the fight, then the actual fight, then the end of the fight, which is the point when someone usually gets badly hurt.

I still can't understand why they enjoy it so much; they are like animals. I look away from the boy, because he looks ashamed and I don't want to add to that by staring at him.

After he's gone, Eadie comes out of the building too.

'How are you, Lesley? How was your day?'

'Good. I went to the library at dinnertime and I'm trying to teach myself Latin.'

'What words did you learn?'

'*Valde bona.*'

'Oh excellent, *bene factum.*'

'Whit was that?'

'I said "well done".'

'Have you heard anything from the Andersons?'

'Sort of.'

'Whit do you mean, sort of? Have they changed their minds?'

'No, no, they haven't changed their minds.'

'Oh great, so it's still going to happen?'

'Shall we go to my office to talk about it?'

'Is something wrong?'

'It's best we talk in private.'

We walk to her office in silence. I already know it's bad news, just not what the bad news is. No one waits to give you good news.

I follow her along the corridor, she unlocks her office, and I walk straight to my chair. She takes her coat off, then sits in her chair and lets out a big sigh.

I want to just shout, 'WHAT IS IT? WHAT NOW?' But I wait.

'All right,' she says, 'there's been a setback in the adoption. In fact, at the moment it looks like it is off.'

'But ... why?'

'It's complicated, I'm afraid.'

'Complicated how? Tell me. I can understand complicated things.'

'I'm afraid I can't right now.'

'Why can't you, if it's me it affects?'

'There are procedures in these situations, so that is all I can say.'

'Just tell me. Please.'

There's a pause. I can see her struggling. Then her face moves as if she's come to a decision. She takes a slow, deep breath, looks straight at me and says, 'Your adoption has been blocked.'

'Why?' I say. 'By who?'

'That is what I cannot tell you, Lesley. Please understand the situation I am in; if I could, I honestly would tell you, but I truly can't.'

She looks angry with me. I have never seen her look angry with me before and I can't understand why. First the adoption gets stopped and now Eadie doesn't even like me. It's the curse of adults again. Adults cause pain.

I get up and run back to the cottage, tears rolling down my face. All I can think is if there is no one I can rely on in this world, then I will have to rely on myself.

64

Life is continuing. I have to continue. I'm struggling to accept that I won't get out of here.

I would rather not have had the chance than have had the chance and have it taken away from me.

The days have turned into weeks and still I haven't gone back to see Eadie. Now it's the first week of a new school year – I was glad to see Clara again when we got back, but it feels like the summer holidays have taken their toll and while everyone else at the grammar school is fresh after the break, I feel exhausted. That's the kind of thing I would usually tell Eadie. I can't trust her now. The one person I thought I could trust and even she won't tell me the truth.

I don't know what happens to you when you become a grown-up, what changes. There's not a single adult who won't let you down or lie or find some other way to make you suffer.

Ever since my mum gave me away at three weeks, I've

been let down by grown-ups. Gran lied about my sisters and brother; the minister lies about God.

And if it's not them lying it's them either trying to do it to us like Mr Taylor, beat us for fun like Mr Paterson, or kill for some terrible reason like whoever the bastard is who killed Jonesy. We are just here so adults can cause us suffering.

Eadie was the one grown-up I thought would never let me down. How many times can people hurt your heart until it just dies?

Is that what makes you into an adult, having been so betrayed that you are dead and no one can hurt you any more and then you don't feel so bad about doing the same to others? Does getting older make you nastier, or do you have to be nasty to get old? Was Jonesy taken away because she was too nice? Does that mean when I'm older I will turn into a person who lies and lets people down and makes them hate me?

I hate grown-ups.

*

I still don't sleep well.

Ever since Jonesy went I either sleep, but have these really bad nightmares, or I can't sleep at all. Or both. I'll sleep, have a nightmare, then not get back to sleep.

I'll sometimes just lie in bed all night, staring at the ceiling, hoping my head will go quiet enough for me to drop off. Or I'll close my eyes and turn over, and keep them tight shut but sleep just won't come.

Mr and Mrs Paterson have always said that we're not allowed out of our rooms at night no matter what, but after Jonesy died Mrs Paterson said if I needed to come see her because I felt scared then I could. She said I should always know that she was just downstairs, so not to be frightened, and if it was getting too bad I could come down and sleep on their sofa.

I occasionally did. The girls in my room didn't know; I would sneak back up to bed before they were up. The first two times I did it I went into Mr and Mrs Paterson's room. Mr Paterson was a bit grumpy, but Mrs Paterson told him to shush.

After the second time Mrs Paterson said she would leave a blanket out for me each night so I needn't wake them; I could just come down and curl up on the settee.

I haven't done it for a few weeks as my sleeping had been getting back to normal but since the news about the Andersons, I have had some terrible nights. My brain won't switch off; it just keeps going over and over what happened. Was it something I did? Why won't anyone tell me the truth?

*

It feels like it's about two in the morning. I don't have a watch but I'm pretty good at guessing the time after waking up so much. I pull back my covers and creep out of the bedroom. The house is totally silent. I make my way down the stairs and into the Patersons' living room.

I walk quietly to the sofa, picking up the blanket from

its place on the chair by the door. The blanket smells musty but I don't mind much and wrap it round me as tight as I can, then lay my head on the cushions.

The room is in half-light. The lamp outside our cottage is shining and the curtains aren't closed so the light comes into the room.

I can hear Mr Paterson snoring from the other room. I've heard it before and know it's him. Mrs Paterson actually snores a little too, but hers is pretty mild compared to him.

His is a weird one-in-every-three snore. He doesn't do it on every breath, or at least I think he doesn't do it on every breath, unless he's a whale. Whales can hold their breath for half an hour. If he is doing it on every breath it means he must breathe only once a minute.

I lie there listening to the sounds, hoping I can drift off. Last time I came down here I spent ages thinking, *How on earth can Mrs Paterson still be asleep lying next to that noise?* Has she got earplugs in? How could anyone put up with that? Anyway, next thing I knew it was morning.

So I listen to the sounds and wonder if Mr Paterson isn't next door but maybe a cow has come in from the field and is sleeping next to Mrs Paterson. It doesn't work this time, I'm not drifting off; my mind keeps going back to Eadie, to the Andersons.

I sit up, keeping the blanket wrapped round me, and shuffle to the chair so I can look out of the window. It's a very still night, no rustling in the trees, no rain. In six hours the village will be alive with the sound of children shrieking, running, fighting, kicking balls, calling names.

I watch as a fox crosses the path. It trots to the lamp-post, and stops as if to look around, then something scares it and it darts off. Then nothing again, stillness.

I try to get comfortable in my upright sitting position. A box near the sofa has some letters on it so I move them onto the floor so I can put my feet up but catch my leg on the edge of the lid. It makes my calf itch so I use the corner of the lid to scratch the itch. It goes, but a minute later it comes back, so I scratch so hard that it won't be able to come back.

It does, so I give up, put my feet down and look at the box. I open it to see inside, just to make sure I'm not putting my feet up on something fragile. It's filled with old newspapers, lots of them. The front page of the top one has the headline GUILTY! MONTROSE TO HANG. It's from the *Evening Times*.

I turn on the light next to me and examine the paper. It's from ten years ago. Beneath it are other newspapers or individual pages from newspapers. They are all about the Peter Montrose murders, the trial and then the hanging.

I read page after page, the details about what he did to those women. Much of it is the same information I read in the library weeks ago, but it's not just one newspaper, there are lots and lots of cuttings from different papers.

I hear a sound from the bedroom, so I quickly turn the light off, shut the box and put the letters back on top. I fold the blanket and put it back in its place on the chair before sneaking up the stairs and into bed.

Now I am never going to sleep; my head is racing with questions.

Why do the Patersons have all those newspaper cuttings? What do the Montrose murders have to do with them?

I stay wide awake for the rest of the night waiting for the morning light to come. I don't go to breakfast and when it's time I leave the house without saying a word to anyone and get straight on the bus for school.

65

At school I can't concentrate. I don't hear what the teachers are saying. All I can think is, *Why would the Patersons have those newspapers?* Was Jonesy right? Did the police get the wrong man, and the real killer wasn't Peter Montrose, but Mr Paterson? Is that why he kept the clippings, so he could gloat that he'd gotten away with it? Maybe Mrs Paterson doesn't know about the clippings, doesn't know she's living with a killer? Or maybe she does know, and she's in on it, too?

Jonesy must have found the newspapers; she always was nosey. That terrible, terrible man; all that time being nicer to me and he knew what he'd done to her.

I borrow some money from Clara and at first break I go to the phone booth to call Detective Walker. He isn't there so I say I will call again at dinnertime, but I don't give my name.

He still isn't there when I call back. This time I say it's very important that I speak to him, but again I don't give my name.

All afternoon I carry on worrying. I have to go back to the cottage and face them.

During maths I say I'm feeling ill and ask to go see the nurse. I never miss maths, but I have to speak to the detective. I sneak to the phone booth and dial the number again. This time he picks up the phone on the second ring.

'Detective Walker, I need to speak to you.'

'Ahh ... Lesley, I imagine?'

'Yes, yes, I need to speak to you.'

'And what is it this time?'

'Mr Paterson, it's Mr Paterson, you know, our house-father at Cottage 5, I think he could be involved in it, perhaps Mrs Paterson too, but I think Mr Paterson might have done it.'

'All riiight ...' he says, stretching it out. 'So why do you say that?'

'Well, he had the opportunity to kill Jonesy, and he probably did Jonesy because she found out it was him, and she found out it was him because she thought that they got the wrong fella for the Montrose murders, and I was in their living room last night and I found lots and lots of newspaper clippings about the Montrose murders. I mean, why would they collect all that stuff? It's obvious, it wasn't Peter Montrose who did the murders, it was Mr Paterson. They hanged the wrong man. I cannae go back there, Detective, I cannae, he'll see in my eyes that I know and he'll do to me what he did to Jonesy.'

There's a long pause, then Detective Walker responds. 'Lesley, where are you?'

'I'm at school.'

'And what time do you finish?'

'Three-thirty.'

'And what time do you get back to the Homes?'

'Six o' clock.'

'Right, here's what is going to happen, Lesley. I am going to meet you back at the Homes, out the front of the executive building. When you get off the bus, do not go back to your cottage, and do not, I repeat, do not, speak to anyone else about this. Do you understand?'

'I understand.'

I knew it was the right thing to call him. He had said before to call if I knew anything and that is what I have done. I know I was wrong about Mr Sharples, but you have to keep asking questions and then you finally work it out.

I think about going to the nurse's office and following through with the lie. There's still twenty minutes of my lesson left, but I decide to go back to the classroom instead. When Mr Sanders asks why I'm back I say I don't feel so bad any more.

I go back to my desk, thinking about what the police will do when they arrest Mr Paterson. Will they arrest Mrs Paterson too? Will I have to move cottages? Will the others in Cottage 5 hate me for getting rid of them? They shouldn't, I might have saved their lives.

66

My heart is raging as I get off the bus. The journey was quicker than usual, so I'm ten minutes early and I stand round the back of the executive building. I watch the other children running around not knowing what I know, not knowing who is living amongst us.

At six exactly I go round to the front and see Detective Walker. He's wearing his suit even though it is a hot day and he walks up to me with a stern look on his face, a look that says I am in trouble.

'We should have a chat,' he says. 'You haven't been back to the cottage, have you?'

I shake my head.

'Good, because there is something important that I need you to know; something you must *never* mention again. Do you understand?'

I nod.

'Shall we go and sit down there?' he says, pointing to the bench by the side of the road. I follow him and do as he says. The bench is slightly damp as it had rained a bit this afternoon, and the sun hasn't quite dried it out yet.

He seems calm, but I can sense that he's angry. I have seen this look in so many adults' eyes.

'Now, explain to me what it was that you found.'

I tell him about the newspaper clippings reporting the Montrose murders, and how Jonesy had wondered whether they had hanged the wrong man and the killer was free to commit more murders, and that is what they're doing now.

Then I say, 'When I saw those newspapers – I mean, why would you keep them if you weren't involved? Then I thought mibbie Jonesy had said something to Mr Paterson and he realised she knew and that's why he killed her.'

'That's what I thought you might have been getting at. Right.' He takes off his jacket. I can see the sweat patches underneath. He breathes twice, deeply; I don't know if he's doing it for show.

'When you work for the police, you learn that when you have a piece of evidence you look for all the different reasons it exists. You don't just pick the first one that comes into your head, or the one that fits your narrative.'

I put my hand up.

'Yes?'

'Whit's a narrative?'

'It's a story. So if you see something important, you don't automatically assume it fits your story in a certain way.'

'So, that's whit I've done?'

'Yes, yes, you have. There could be another reason for the Patersons having those clippings.'

'And there is?'

'Yes there is, Lesley. There is a reason, but I need you to swear, and I mean swear *on your life*, that you will not tell a soul what I am just about to tell you.' He looks me straight in the eye and I know it's serious. 'How much do you know about the Peter Montrose murders?'

'I know he killed eight women.'

Detective Walker nods. 'Yes. There's a bit more to it than that but, yes, he was convicted of killing eight women, although many of us think he killed nine. There were also two women whom he attacked but who managed to escape, and they gave evidence against him. One of those women was Mrs Paterson, or, as she was known back then, Miss McKinley. She was attacked by Peter Montrose and she gave evidence that ultimately led to him being convicted. For that, the police force are very grateful to her.

'So, Lesley, I would assume that is why she has those newspaper cuttings. No doubt, it has been a traumatic time for her, with these recent deaths. It's hard when you've been through something like that.'

I feel awful, and though I try not to, I start to cry. He puts his arm round me and that makes me sob even more.

'I'm sorry, Mr Walker. I'm really sorry. I just thought it was Mr Paterson, and he can get angry sometimes and, whit with whit happened, and – he doesnae know, does he? *She* doesnae know whit I said to you?'

'Not yet. That's why I wanted to meet you here first,

before you had a chance to go back to your cottage and tell anyone. Though I'm afraid I will have to let them know eventually.'

'I didn't mean anything, I just thought—'

'Lesley, it's natural ... You are a smart girl; you're always going to be looking for answers. It's just that this time you were wrong. It's what we would call an "avenue of investigation" – you follow up a theory to its end. That way you can rule them out and eventually you'll reach the avenue that leads you to the guilty person. We questioned all the housefathers and other men who work at the Homes after the murders to confirm their alibis, including Mr Paterson.'

'Whit's an alibi?'

'It's when someone can prove that they weren't in the place where the murder happened when it happened.'

'And Mr Paterson has alibis for Jane and Sally and Jonesy? That means he cannae have done it.'

Detective Walker smiles at me. 'That's correct, Lesley. You catch on quick. I think you could make a good detective one day.'

'You said that before. Do you really think so?'

'Sure, you've got brains, you're inquisitive. If one good thing came out of all this, it's that some day we could have you on the police force. Now, let me walk you back to the cottage to show there's no hard feelings.'

Walking back, I forget about feeling guilty and am full of the idea that I could become a police detective. None of them seem to be women but Detective Walker thinks I could be one. I could solve other murders. Science is over for me. This is what I am going to become.

At the steps to Cottage 5 he says, 'So, we are all right?'

'We are all right,' I say.

We shake hands like grown-ups.

As I watch him walk off, I decide two things: I'm going to be a detective when I'm older, and I am going to solve this case once and for all, and they will see that I will make a great detective.

I haven't made a mistake. I have eliminated a suspect. I am closer to finding out the truth.

67

I have forgiven Eadie. It's not her fault that the adoption was blocked. And she must have her reasons for not telling me who did it. I do believe she is a good person; she wouldn't have done that to me if she could have helped it. I shouldn't have been so hard on her.

It's Saturday so I decide to go to my morning meeting with her. My usual time is 10 a.m. but I head over now at quarter to as sometimes she finishes early with the kid before me, so I get to have more than half an hour.

The hospital smells different to all the other buildings in the Homes. The church smells of dust and damp, the big hall smells of sweaty boys, who often have games there, but the hospital smells like disinfectant.

I head up the first flight of stairs towards her office. Her door is shut, so I sit outside. Sometimes if she is somewhere else in the building the room is locked and I just wait; she's never too late.

I sit and read the notices on the wall. At twenty past

she still hasn't arrived and I start to get a little worried. She never doesn't show up. I wait another hour, and still nothing.

There's no note on the door. A couple of grown-ups walk past and I ask them if they've seen her and they say no.

At half-past eleven I decide to go looking for one of the nurses. When I find one, she says that Eadie won't be coming back. I ask her why and she says she couldn't say.

I am annoyed that she won't tell me why Eadie is away but also glad that there is a reason she isn't here; I was worried that something had happened to her. It seems to be how my mind works now.

Although I've skipped a few meetings because I was annoyed with Eadie, I never meant for it to be for so long. Now I know that I need my time with her each week – I rely on it. I sit back down and try to work out why she has gone, work through the avenues that might explain it. My immediate reaction was that she'd been killed, but I need to train myself like Detective Walker said; think through all the possibilities. If she had known she was going to leave she would have told me, she would have told all of us, so she must have left suddenly without knowing beforehand.

I remember that Glenda sees Eadie too, so I run over to her cottage. She's hanging around with her little crew. I nod at her and she nods back, then I flick my head to the side, to mean, *Come this way*. She starts walking with me and her friends come too. She stops and looks at them and shakes her head, and that's all it takes for them to stop where they are. She has such control over her friends it's amazing.

'Whit's goin' on?' she says.

'You seen Eadie?'

'Aye, Thursday. Why, whit's happened?'

'She's gone.'

'Gone? How so?'

'Gone. Nurse says she's no coming back.'

Her face looks how I feel. 'She cannae be gone.'

'She is so, no message for us, no nothing.'

'Tha's no fair,' she says. Glenda doesn't look angry, just hurt. 'Someone has to have got rid of her. She's too nice to run oot on us.'

'I know, but who?'

'Bastard Super, that's who.'

'No.'

'Aye, he never liked her, I can tell.'

'Aye, but not enough to get rid of her.'

We've reached the edge of the woods and stop.

'Whit we gonnae do?' she asks.

'We're gonnae find out who knows why Eadie's gone, then we're gonnae find out why she's gone, then we're gonnae get her back.'

'Aye right,' says Glenda, nodding.

'Right,' I say.

She walks back to her cottage and I walk back to mine. *That bastard Super*, I think. *He must know, for sure.*

68

I'm in the kitchen on my own after school. I've just finished the crumble and custard that Cook left out for my tea.

The moment I finish the last spoonful Mrs Paterson taps me on the shoulder. I didn't hear her come in. 'Can I speak to you for a moment?' she says.

I sense trouble but I stand up and walk after her into her sitting room. 'Sit down,' she says, and I do.

I have the feeling I get when I know I'm going to get told off. I feel like I'm frozen and can't move, but I have to.

She sits down next to me and puts her knees together. 'Do you see my fringe?' she asks, pointing at her hair. 'Have you ever seen my forehead?'

I shake my head. I never have seen it as she always wears her hair the same way, ponytail at the back and fringe at the front. She lifts the fringe up, revealing her forehead and, up by the hairline, a four-inch jagged scar.

'Do you see this?' I nod. 'It was done by Peter Montrose.

The other scars are behind my hairline so no one can see them, but I have to hide this one.

'It's not a nice story. He dragged me off the side of the road behind some bushes and hit me with the hammer. He hit me so hard my skull was fractured in three places. He didn't manage to knock me out, though he thought he had. As I was lying on the ground, he started to pull at my dress so I kicked him, as hard as I have ever kicked anyone in my life, then I staggered out into the road and was saved by the driver of a passing car. So that's what happened. And I keep those newspapers because I want to be sure they got him, and I want to be sure they hanged him. And when I get scared or have nightmares, I read them again. That is why I keep them. Do you understand?'

'Yes, miss,' I say.

'And I don't want you ever snooping through our belongings again. We let you sleep downstairs because you have had a hard time, but don't try it on, Lesley.'

'Yes, miss,' I say, drenched in shame.

'Also, Lesley ...'

'Yes, miss?'

'There's something else I want to talk to you about.'

The shame is now joined by fear as I wonder what else I could have done wrong.

'The Andersons, the adoption – I wanted to talk to you about that.'

I look at her eyes to try to guess what she is going to say. I feel relief as I know nothing can hurt me any more with regard to the adoption, I've already had the worst news I could get. This is something I've learnt this summer;

sometimes things are so bad that it's simply impossible for them to get any worse.

'I gather no one has told you why it was stopped.'

I nod.

'I think that is unfair, Lesley. So I'm going to tell you, but you are not to tell anyone. Do you understand?'

I nod again.

'It was your mother. Your mother put a stop to the adoption; she says that she still wants the option to take you to live with her. If you go with the Andersons then you are unlikely ever to be reunited with your real family. So what she's done in cancelling it, she's done from a good place. She wants you back with her.'

'But I dinnae want to go with her,' I say. 'I want to be with the Andersons.' I try to breathe slowly. 'If she wanted me to live with her she's had years to do that, or is it only now someone else wants me? Why did she change her mind? What about what *I* want?'

'She's your mother, Lesley, and until you are sixteen, she gets a say.'

'Sixteen is ages away. Sixteen means I'm stuck here for ever.'

'It will go quickly, Lesley, I promise.'

'Well, the moment I'm sixteen I'm choosing never to see her again.'

'I understand.'

'What about the Andersons? Whit did they say?'

'They were obviously disappointed, they really liked you and were hoping it could be worked out, but ultimately they understood.'

I nod again. 'Can I go now?' I say.

'Yes, Lesley.'

I go upstairs to my room. The girls are all in there talking. I lie down on my bed and look at the wall. The others barely notice.

My head has too many thoughts in it again. To be wanted by someone you don't want to be wanted by. By someone who you did want to want you way back, but now you don't want them to want you and it's only now that they do want you. The people who do want you and you want back can't have you.

Is this going to be my life?

69

It's nearly time for tea when I hear the scream.

I'm sat on the front steps of Cottage 5 with Shona, Eldrey, Mary and Pam. Shona is saying that she has a boyfriend, but won't say who. Mary is begging to know who it is. Eldrey is staring off into space. Pam doesn't believe Shona and I don't know what to think.

The scream comes from Cottage 8, which is Glenda McAdam's house. It sounds like it's her doing the screaming. First I hear, 'Noooooo!' followed by, 'Daddy!'

I can see her out the front of her house. Her friends are standing in the doorway but she's on the grass. There's a man walking away, a big heavyset man, and it's more of a stagger than a walk. It's her dad. He's back again and he's drunk again.

I look at Glenda stood there. You can see she doesn't know whether to go after him or not. From what I've seen and heard, I would advise her to stay away. He is a bad, angry, dangerous man; Jonesy said so before.

I talk to Glenda more now that Eadie isn't about. She

appreciated Eadie as much as I did. We both really miss her and are sad she has gone. Glenda doesn't know why she's gone either, but she's promised to tell me if she finds anything out. Sometimes when we talk, she mentions her dad and the drink, and how scared he can make her.

Pam runs over to Cottage 8 then runs back. She tells us that apparently he's come for the eldest McAdam lad. It seems there was an insult to the mother and now the dad is going to batter him.

Glenda is still stood there on her own, no one has gone to her, so eventually I walk over. I think the girls from Cottage 5 are a bit shocked as they still think she's my mortal enemy; they don't know that we've been talking and, although we're not friends, we do get on.

'Y'all right, Glen?' I say.

'Nuh.'

'Da gone crazy again?'

'Aye,' she says, kind of resigned. 'Been drinking again, said he's gonnae kill Tommy, says he's said something to Ma and he has to pay. I asked him what Tommy said. He said it disnae matter. I think he can't remember, just wants to crack a heid.'

'How long's this gonnae go on?'

'Till one of the boys gets big enough to batter him back, I suppose. Or he drinks himself to death. No great options, eh?'

'Anyone called the polis?' I ask.

''Spect so, someone usually does. Just a case of whether they get to him afore he gets to Tommy.'

'Should we try to stop him?'

'No worth it, we'd only end up getting a battering too.'

We stand there looking in the direction Mr McAdam walked off in.

'Shall we go back inside?' I ask.

'Feels sorta wrong to, knowing my da is rampaging about.'

'Aye. Well, I'm off back to our cottage. Come over if you want to.'

'Thanks, I'll stay here for a bit,' she says.

'Right,' I say, and walk back to Pam and the girls. Soon we get called in for tea.

*

At the table, the girls ask me how come I'm friends with Glenda now. I explain that we aren't friends, but we have a sort of understanding and chat sometimes. They seem shocked. It makes me happy that I have surprised them. I haven't surprised anyone in a long time.

After tea Glenda does come over. The doorbell rings and Mrs Paterson answers it; she doesn't want to let her in, but I beg, so she says she can stay 'five minutes, but not a moment longer'.

Turns out the police did get Glenda's da, but only after he tried to batter Tommy; only he couldn't, he was too drunk, apparently. Tommy stayed out of striking distance and danced around him while he swung punches and shouted curses.

As someone who doesn't have a dad, I have been jealous in the past of people who have one, but as I've learnt, having one that's bad is worse than not having one at all. This is where not having one isn't so bad.

Poor Glenda. I think I'm starting to like her; she's not the person everyone thinks she is. When you get to know her she's actually good, I just don't think she's ever been able to show it.

That evening I can't stop thinking about Glenda's father. Imagine having someone that dangerous as your dad. Imagine not knowing if he was going to be nice or crazy when he visited; it sounds like he was never a nice man. It's no wonder they took the kids away. Glenda is probably safer here.

70

This is me, this is where my life is.

I am twelve years old. I have two sisters and a brother. I have never met them, I don't know if they know I exist. I have a mother who put me in an orphanage when I was three weeks old, who won't let me get adopted because she wants me to live with her family but hasn't done anything about it.

It looks like I have another three or four years in this place till I get to leave and I cannot wait. I did have Eadie, the one person I could rely on in here, but she is now gone.

I am basically alone. I have friends, but not great friends. I have Clara at school, and the girls in my room, but no one as close as Jonesy who was killed at the back of the house which I still have to live in. Two other girls were killed. Someone in the Homes probably did it but no one knows who and the police don't care about finding them.

People seem to have gone back to normal. I can't understand how. This isn't right, I am not the same person I was at the start of the summer.

If the police don't find the murderer, then are they just hoping it will all go away? Why aren't they doing more? Why aren't police about here all the time until the killer is caught?

My aim is just to get through each day, and if enough days go by, eventually I can leave. But only if the murderer doesn't come back and attack me. If no one seems capable of finding out who killed Jonesy, then I need to find who did it – the adults do not seem able. Finding out who killed her is the quickest way to me being safe. I can stop being scared and get revenge for Jonesy.

Mr Sharples is weird and creepy, but the police say he didn't do it. Mr Taylor can't have done it – even though he was going with Jane Denton, which was bad – as he was in custody when Sally Ward got killed, and he'd already been sent away when what happened to Jonesy happened. He can't have come back just to kill Jonesy, or someone would have noticed him sneaking about – someone sees most things around here. The McAdams' da is too much of a drunk to be able to do it even though he is a terrible man. He'd be more likely to do that to one of his *own* kids, not one he didn't know.

I thought Mr Paterson could have done it as he can be nasty and Jonesy lived in his cottage and because of the newspapers. But Detective Walker said he couldn't have done it because he had alibis, and now I know why the Patersons have all those clippings about Peter Montrose, it was about Mrs Paterson, not Mr Paterson. Besides, Mr Paterson wouldn't have spoken to Jane Denton in years or known who Sally Ward was.

It must be someone around here, but who? Adults don't have the answers. When you ask them about God, they lie; when you ask them for the truth, they can't tell you. You have to find your own answers, not take their word for it.

I need to speak to Eadie about this. There is one person who will know why she has gone and when she is coming back. I don't want to speak to him as he scares me but he's the only one who will have real answers. He will know what's happened to Eadie, and he will know about the investigation.

I set off down Hope Avenue. I am walking quickly. Some girls say hello but I don't hear them until I have passed. I go into the executive building up the big stairs and I walk up to the secretary who is sat in front of a desk outside his office.

She looks tidy and proper, like she went to a school for manners.

'How can I help you, young lady?' she says, peering over her glasses.

'I need to see the Superintendent.'

'I'm sure you do but Mr Gordon is a busy man.'

'I know, miss, but it's very important.'

'Could you let me know what matter it relates to?'

'I cannae, miss, I cannae say anything, I have to tell him in person, please, miss, trust me.'

'Young lady, what is your name?'

'Lesley.'

'Right Lesley, my job here is to assist the Superintendent and one of the ways I do that is by not letting people bother him unless it's absolutely necessary.'

'But it is, miss, it is,' I say, louder.

The door to his office opens and Mr Gordon sticks his head out and gruffly asks, 'What's going on?'

'Ah Superintendent, I was just explaining to this young lady that it was not possible—'

My chance is slipping. She will talk me out of seeing him. I can see his granite face with the pockets under his eyes, his hard bald head and tight grey buttoned-up shirt.

'Sir, sir,' I cut in. 'I need to talk to you, sir, it's important.'

'Very well, come in,' he says, just like that.

I nod at the secretary to say, *See?* and she gives me a look back like she's chewing a nettle.

I follow the Superintendent into his office. The window looks out to the main gates and there is a map of the Homes on his wall. The large desk is stacked with papers. I can smell the authority in the room. He controls everything at the Homes from here, and if you are ever sent to see the Superintendent you know you are in for a world of sorrow.

His punishments are legendary. Rumour is, he's even given a couple of the housefathers a doing over their failure to control their houses. That's why the housefathers can be so strict, cos if they don't they are going to get it from him. It's a pyramid of beatings and we are at the bottom.

I feel terrified being in the room alone with him.

Mr Gordon points to the chair for me to sit down, and he takes his seat behind the desk, then leans forward.

'I know you,' he says, and my heart sinks. 'You're one

of the girls in the Patersons' house, aren't you? Cottage 5? And you go to the grammar school?'

I nod.

'I believe you had a fight with Glenda McAdams last term, did you not?'

I nod again. 'How did you know?'

'It's my job to know everything that goes on in this place. I gather that you managed to emerge victorious, which is some feat. And it was your friend, young Morag Jones, who sadly died at the start of the summer holidays, correct?'

I nod again.

'What is your name?'

'Lesley, sir. Lesley Beaton.'

'Ah that's right, I knew it would come back to me. So, what is so urgent that you need to see me?'

'Sir, where's Eadie Schaffer gone? I'm worried about her.'

'She's fine. She's just had to leave, I'm afraid.'

'But why, sir?'

'The why is none of your business.'

'But she's just gone, without saying anything, she would have said something. Will she be back?'

'I don't think so, no.'

This hurts. It was bad to lose her, but to not have the hope that she will come back hurts more. I am tired of hurting.

'Was there anything else?'

I try to compose myself and say what I need to say.

'Well?'

'Why haven't the polis caught whoever it is killing girls? I mean, how hard can it be? How hard are they trying? At first I thought it was Mr Sharples; he's strange, he has mental problems. But the polis say it isn't him.'

'I'm aware of your suspicions, but I can assure you that Mr Sharples was not responsible for any of the murders. He could account for his whereabouts for each time.'

'Then I thought it was Mr Paterson. There are all these newspaper clippings about the Montrose murders in the sitting room at the cottage and I thought he could have done it, being Morag's housefather. But then Detective Walker told me that he had alibis and about Mrs Paterson and I felt awful. At one point me and Morag even wondered if it was Glenda McAdam's dad. But I don't think it couldae been him. So who did it? They are still out there, why is no one doing anything?'

I sound angry. I don't mean to, but I can't help it.

'Lesley, the police have a huge team on it, we are doing all we can do.'

'But we're no safe. While the murderer is still out there we're no safe.'

'I assure you, you *are* all safe.'

And then I make my mistake.

'But we're not,' I say. 'You say we are, but girls are dying. My friend died, I could be next, and it must be someone at the Homes, someone who is here every day and they could murder another girl at any time. The polis can't seem to find them, so mibbie someone is telling them lies to send them in the wrong direction so the killer is free to do it again. And the person who speaks to the polis the most is you!'

There is silence in the room. The Superintendent stares straight at me.

'You're the one who can go anywhere in the grounds and not be suspicious. You can tell the polis the wrong thing. You can pretend to keep us safe and all the time have us where you can get us. It's you. It's you, you killed Jonesy!'

I find myself shouting, and I realise what I have just said, and I want to pull it back into my mouth, but it hangs between us and I know I am in more trouble than I have ever been in before.

His face goes red, steaming red. His nostrils flare.

'What did you just say?'

'Sir, I'm sorry, sir, I'm so, so sorry.'

'Sorry? I'm going to make you sorry. Miss McArdle, get this girl out of here.'

The door opens behind me and the secretary is stood there. I run out as fast as I can. I think he might try to grab me, and if gets me he will try to kill me, he has to, I know his secret.

I went in there thinking he was a bastard and came out knowing it. He doesn't care about the Homes children, he doesn't even like them, he thinks we are rats.

And we are. I scurry down the stairs, and race back to my cottage. We are little things he has to control to make sure we don't cause trouble.

As I run back it comes to me, like a vision, clarity. Like Detective Walker said, you look at all angles and from one angle you can see the answer – and I see it.

We have to get away.

71

I get back to Cottage 5. I need to speak to Mrs Paterson. I need to tell her that we are in trouble.

She's talking to some of the bigger girls, telling them off for something one of the girls has done in their bedroom and how all of them will be held responsible. The girls look like they just want the telling off to end, but Mrs Paterson keeps going. I can't wait much longer.

Eventually she ends with: 'So if you do that again, there is going to be serious trouble, do you understand?' The older girls' shoulders relax as they realise it is finally over and not that serious. At least Mr Paterson hasn't been involved.

As soon as Mrs Paterson is finished, I run up to her.

'Miss, I need to talk to you. It's urgent.'

'Can it wait, Lesley? I need to get some things for the house right now.'

I can tell she is starting to tire of me, how much work I am since Jonesy died. I can see it in her expression; when she turned around and saw it was me her smile faded a little. But I need to really stress how much danger we are in, and for her to take me seriously. I am done with not having adults listen to me, or pretending they are listening to me then ignoring what I say.

'No, miss, this cannae wait, I need your help, I need it now.'

She looks at me and I can tell she's thinking, *Is this another one of her stupid wee ideas or is this something genuinely important I have to listen to?*

I stare at her. I try to put on my most serious face so she knows I'm not messing.

We are by the front door and suddenly I see through one of the glass panels that the Superintendent is walking towards the cottage. He looks really angry. I know he's coming for me, or to tell the Patersons what I just accused him of.

'Quick!' I say. 'He's coming!' and I grab Mrs Paterson's arm and drag her through the kitchen and out the back door just as I hear three loud bangs on the front door.

'Wait! Stop! Who's coming?' she asks.

'Mr Gordon, miss, he's coming for me.'

'What? Why is he coming for you? Why are we running?'

We go around the side of the house and I can hear the front door being opened and the Super shouting, 'WHERE ARE THE PATERSONS?'

'Quick, follow me,' I say, and I'm pleased that she comes with me without asking any more questions. We scuttle across the green, towards the church. Soon we are out of sight of the cottage. Mrs Paterson is breathing heavily, and we slow down to a walk when we get into the woods.

'What is going on, Lesley? What have you got me doing?'

I stop. We're near where Jane's body was found. I stand by a tree and put my arm against it to compose myself.

'Miss, I think it's him. I think Mr Gordon is the murderer. He can go everywhere, he can steer the polis in the wrong direction, he's got access to every cottage, he hates us kids, he could be seen with anyone and it no be suspicious, he's made Eadie disappear. Has he killed her? No one seems to be able to tell me where she is.

'I went to see him about Eadie but then I started to go on about how no one is doing anything and it clicked, and I told him I think it was him that killed the girls, and that's why he's come to the house because he knows I'm right and he's gonnae try to do me in, miss! And you're no safe either as he might think that I've told you and then he'll have to get rid of you too. Miss, it was him all along! He was the bastard who killed Jonesy and I'm no safe in the house any more as he knows where I sleep and I can't tell Detective Walker as he doesnae trust me any more as I got those other people wrong and no one is gonnae stop him and I'm gonnae be the next one deid.'

My brain is working so fast I'm not sure I'm making sense, but I can't seem to stop.

'But why would the Super kill Eadie? Whit's she ever done to anyone but help them, and why would he kill Jonesy? Or Jane or Sally? I cannae tell the polis. Mibbie you should tell the polis, mibbie they will listen to you.

Will you tell Mr Paterson? He could help us; he could drive us somewhere. Could you drive me to the Andersons? They could look after me ... Or my mum, you could tell her I'm sorry ... Or my gran, she's better – can we call my gran? She could come get me and look after me for a while, just a while, I promise I'll come back when it's safe. I won't run away, I promise, miss ... miss ... I just need help to get away.'

I can't seem to breathe properly. I am trying but I can't seem to get any air into my lungs and I'm dizzy and my face feels fuzzy like it's electric.

Mrs Paterson is looking at me. She is bent down and she is looking directly into my eyes and she is saying something but it is slurred, her words are slow.

Why are her words so slow ... my lips are tingling ... and ... I can't ...

72

The first thing I notice is the smell of bleach. I was in the woods but now I am somewhere with bleach and strong soap.

I open my eyes and the room is very white. It hurts to look at it. Something has happened. I am in a bed in the hospital.

I'm not injured, nothing seems to hurt on my body, I haven't been beaten, I am lying in a bed with the sheets tucked tight, holding me in.

I look to my right and Mrs Paterson is sat on a chair and is holding my hand.

'Are you all right, dear? Are you back with us?'

I nod.

'You had a little episode, Lesley. You collapsed and we brought you to the hospital.'

I nod again.

I hear the squeaks of a trolley going past in the corridor outside.

We sit and don't talk for a while.

'Have you had anything to eat or drink today? The doctors think you may be dehydrated. There's a sandwich and a glass of milk here for you, and they have given you a sedative, too, to help you relax.'

I nod.

'Lesley, you have had an awful lot of terrible things happen to you this summer and I guess we didn't notice how much, what with your mum and the adoption, and Morag, and now Eadie going. It's a lot for anyone to take in.'

'But the Super? Does he know where I am?'

'He helped carry you here, Lesley. Mr Gordon is not a bad man. Believe me, he is the last person who would have done all the things you said. You thought it was Mr Taylor – I know it was you who told the police about him; I found the first version of your letter in the rubbish – then you thought it was Mr Sharples or Mr McAdam. You even thought it was Mr Paterson at one point? And now you think it's Mr Gordon. Lesley, you have to realise that this is something you can't work out. It's not a maths puzzle to be solved. The world doesn't work like that.

'Sometimes you just need your brain to go quiet for a bit, not let it rule you. You are a special girl, Lesley, with a special mind that will help you do many things in life, but remember it works for you; you don't work for it.'

'Yes, miss.'

She squeezes my hand.

'They have said you can have this room on your own for the next couple of days, so you don't have to be on the ward with the other children. I need to go back to Cottage 5 now but you just take your time. Rest, sleep, let yourself slow down.'

I nod.

'And eat that sandwich, all right? I want you back to your old self in a few days' time. No rush, but we want the old Lesley back.'

I think I want that old Lesley back too. I was happy before this summer. Well, not always happy but I wasn't always scared, and I had Jonesy and I would give anything to feel like that again.

Mrs Paterson gets up and leaves and I take three bites of my sandwich, drink some milk and stare out of the window at the tops of the trees.

I feel myself getting drowsy again and close my eyes.

73

'Would you like something to eat, doll? Wee bit o' sausage and tatties?'

...

'Just checking your pulse, my love, nothing to worry about.'

...

'Freshening up your water, doll. You keep your eyes shut.'

...

'She's no awake at the moment.'
'Well, let me be the judge of that.'

...

'Lesley? Lesley?'
'Super, she's clearly asleep.'

*

I wake up.

Fear grips me as I open my eyes to see that Mr Gordon is stood at the end of my bed.

'See,' he says turning to the nurse, 'I told you she was awake.'

The nurse walks off. I don't want her to, I don't feel safe with just him and me in this room.

He stays at the end of the bed.

'Lesley, I wanted to check you are all right. Let's forget what was said in my office. I understand you are confused.'

I say nothing.

'I was one of the first people the police interviewed. As a man with access to all areas of the Homes, naturally the police needed to eliminate me from their enquiries, which they have done, for all three deaths. When Jane died, and then when her close friend Sally died, we were all wondering who was responsible. And then of course, your poor pal, Morag.

'No one has been more worried about you children. It is not just my job, but my duty to make sure you are all safe. Not being able to do that has been appalling. Anyway, I just wanted to come here to check on you, and explain the situation to you.'

I nod but say nothing. The nurse walks back in. 'Are you done with her, Super? She really needs her rest.'

'Yes, I am. Look after this lassie, she's a special one.'

He leaves the room and the nurse comes closer.

'OK, sit up, young lady, and take this medicine ... just pop it in your mouth ... sip of water ... another sip. There you go, all done ... back down for some rest.'

*

I stare at the ceiling, and I think about what the Super said, how bad it had all been for him.

He said they had been close friends.

I didn't know Jane and Sally had been *close* friends. Some of the kids had said they were pals, but there were so many different rumours and stories. How close were they?

I feel sleepy.

If they *were* good friends, then Sally probably knew what Jane knew. And Sally was probably killed for what she knew.

So it wasn't random. They were killed for a reason. The police must know this, but not what the reason is.

So Jonesy must have been killed for a reason, too. The same reason.

Not just some man wanting to kill girls. Jonesy must have known something they knew.

My eyes are heavy.

I try to keep them open. I must keep them open. I had it all wrong.

*

'Switching your lights out now. Nurse is on the ward if you need anything.'

*

Jonesy, what did you know?

'... there is such a thing as being too clever, Lesley. Ever heard the phrase "no one likes a smart-arse"? That's the one you need to understand.'

I feel my hand being held and stroked, and I know this voice and it belongs to Mrs Paterson, except it's not the posh voice she usually has. She sounds more like us kids, like this is the real her. My eyes are still heavy, and I keep them shut.

'You always were a special one, and it's no your fault, it's the way you were born. You're too clever and it's got you into trouble. You're like a wee dog with a bone, you. Dinnae know when to just leave it.

'It's none of our faults either. *We* weren't interfering with that girl Jane years back. He does it, and I'm left to pick up the pieces. He's sick. He knows it, too, it's why he drinks. But he doesnae stop it, it's inside him, and I'm the one whit's got to stop it getting found out or we're gone.

'And once Jane was gone, her pal Sally comes along. Stupid lassie asks me for help. Tells me she thinks Malcolm killed Jane to stop her talking, that she knows he'd messed with Jane and that we had to tell the polis. Well, no if I have anything to do with it, you willnae.

'It always comes down to the same thing, it always comes down to them or me, and it's no going to be me. I never wanted you to become one of them. I always liked you, but after what you've done I have no choice. You're trouble. Just like yer little pal. It wasnae her fault either. She overheard me shouting at Malcolm, telling him what I had done, telling him it was his fault I had to do it. She should never have come back at dinnertime, she should have stayed at school. But there she was, standing in the hallway. She heard the lot. She ran, but no quick enough.

'It wasnae her fault, it's no your fault, and it's no my fault. It's just the way it is. But I cannae have you taking this away from me. I got away from Montrose, I'm safe here, and I'm no having you destroy that.'

I open my right eye just the tiniest amount. I don't want her to know I am awake. I can feel her holding my hand and though what I see is blurry and the room is dark, she seems to be looking down at my hand, not at my face. It is very late, or it could even be so late it's early.

I know I am in danger. I know I have to get out of here, away from her, but I am stuck. The bedsheets are tightly tucked in around me. I won't be able to get out in one quick move. I need to loosen the sheets – but how, without her knowing I am awake?

She's still talking. She keeps saying she's sorry. Then she stands up.

I can feel her moving up against the side of my bed.

'I'm sorry, I'm sorry,' she keeps saying.

I open my eyes, pull my arm back, and jab at her face with outstretched fingers. I catch her right between the eye and the nose with everything I have.

She yelps and recoils back, and I am already pulling at the sheets to free my legs and then I am running to the door. I open it and run down the ward to the nurses' desk. It's dark as anything with just a small half-light showing me where to go.

There is no one at the nurses' desk. Behind me I can hear Mrs Paterson coming so I make a right and go down the flights of stairs until I am in the bottom corridor. Still there's no one about and no lights on.

I head for the main entrance. If they lock it at night I am done for, but it is the only exit I know from here.

I hit it at speed and it opens and I am out into the night. It's cold, my breath is steaming out and I need to work out where to go.

Think, Lesley, think.

But I can't. I can't work out who or where to run to; I just need to find someone who can help me, but the Homes are asleep and everything is still.

Mrs Paterson comes flying out the doors behind me. 'Get back here, you wee shite!' she shouts and I run, and all I can think of is Cottage 5, run back to Cottage 5, and I am running barefoot on the path then on the grass and my nightie is getting wet from the ground and I'm running as fast as I can and I am pulling away from her.

I cut across the grass, behind Cottage 32 and then back along the path but I'm slowing, and I can feel myself slowing and I have to keep going.

Eventually I get to Hope Avenue and I can see Cottage 5 and I run for it, and I know the front door will be locked as it always is at night but I head for it anyway and I'm going to make as much noise as I can.

I get to the front door and I bang on it with my fist

– *bang, bang, bang, bang* – and shout, 'Hello! Wake up, anyone!'

I know Mrs Paterson will catch up with me soon. If she gets to me before someone opens the door, I am finished.

No one comes, no lights go on, so I run round to the back door to the kitchen. Sometimes they forget to lock it. I step on something sharp and the pain shoots up my leg but I don't let out a noise in case Mrs Paterson is close by. I get to the back door and I can see Mr Paterson sat at the table by the wall, his head resting on his hand. He seems to be asleep again. I try the door gently and it's locked, but I know some of the older girls have hidden a spare key under a plant pot in case they come back really late.

I bend down to find the pot, lift it up and feel underneath for a key. There is nothing there. If I go to the front door again and bang on it, I will eventually wake Mr Paterson up; if I stay—

An arm grabs me around my neck from behind. 'You stupid girl. You stupid, stupid girl!' she spits.

And she's squeezing my neck, tighter, and she's growling, and I can't breathe.

I ... can't ... get ... any ... air.

Then she let's go, but it's only to spin me around and push me to the ground and kneel on me. And she starts choking me again, she's using her two thumbs on my neck this time, and I'm fighting to push her away and I'm trying to scratch her arms and pull them off but she's too strong and I'm going to die and I'm going to die where Jonesy died and I can't fight any more, oh Jesus this is it, this is where it ends, and it wasn't supposed to end so soon and I had things to do and I was going to make it out of here and her eyes are burning into me and pushing and pushing on my neck and I can't hold out any—

She stops, and the pressure stops and she releases my throat, lets out a grunt and then slumps on top of me.

There is a thud as her skull hits the path beside my head.

I am desperately trying to get air in, but the weight of her body is pinning me down. I can just see blood dribbling out of her mouth; warm liquid is splattered on the side of my face.

I look up and see Cook standing there, holding the biggest knife in the house.

She reaches down and rolls Mrs Paterson off me.

I am on my back with my breath steaming into the air. My neck aches like it's a rag that has been twisted dry.

Cook kneels down next to me.

'You all right, doll?' she says.

I cough, and wheeze and nod. I am not sure I can speak. I think she has broken my throat. A husky growl comes out.

I turn my head to the right, and I can see through the open kitchen door that Mr Paterson is still asleep at the table, oblivious to what has happened yards away.

'I never liked her,' says Cook. 'There was something no right about them two. Always something strange about them, but nobody listens to me, nobody listens to Cook. I could see something wasnae right. I can tell. I can sense bad'uns.'

'What do we do now?' I manage to say.

'Get the Super,' she says. 'Explain what happened. Get the polis here. Get that bastard arrested.' She nods towards the kitchen.

She seems worryingly calm for a person who has just killed someone.

I look around to see if anyone is about, or if any lights have come on at the windows.

Nothing.

We are the only two people awake in the whole village. Mrs Paterson's body lies at our feet. Where there was rage there is now stillness, other than the pool of her blood getting larger and larger, soaking into her hair.

Cook walks quietly into the kitchen, turns the light off, then comes out and shuts the back door, leaving Mr Paterson asleep.

Then we walk together, my bare feet on the grass again and the cold breeze on my legs.

My heart is just slowing down.

'I dinnae trust him, and I didnae ever trust her,' she says. 'I seen his eyes when he looked at the young girls. He is a bad man, and she knew it too.'

'I think she killed Jane,' I croak.

Cook shrugs. 'Could be. The lassie used to live here, did you know that?'

I nod. 'When I was little.'

'She got her moved out when she was about nine. I knew something was up. It was Mrs Paterson whit decided she had to go. One day she just says she's no staying in this house no more, and she got moved.'

We continue walking. The lampposts are lighting the way towards the Super's house. His place is next door to the executive building. He will be angry at being woken up but he's the only one we can tell, and he'll have to call the police.

'Thank you,' I say, 'for saving me.'

'It's no bother,' she replies. 'Ah wisnae sleeping much, mibbie I knew something was up?'

'Well if you hadnae, I'd be deid by now.'

She puts her arm round me as we walk. 'Aye, and we cannae be having that for wee Brainbox. That's your name, y'know.'

'Is that what they call me?'

'Oh, aye.'

'We only call you Cook.'

'I know.'

'What's your real name?'

'It's Morag, like your pal.'

We carry on walking in silence, then we reach the Super's house and Morag bangs hard on the door six times.

74

A few days after everything, Mr Gordon comes to see me. We have a new housemother and housefather, Mr and Mrs McKelpie. They used to run another Homes cottage but retired a few years ago. They have been brought back temporarily until the Superintendent can find someone permanent to look after us. Another change is that Eldrey has been moved to another cottage. No one will tell us why, and she hasn't been to school since.

'Les!' shouts one of the older girls. 'It's the Super, for you.'

Two months ago if I had found out the Super was here to see me I would have turned cold inside, but now things have changed. I walk down the stairs and he says, 'Get your shoes on, I'm going to take you for a walk.' His voice is gentler than it usually is.

I can feel the eyes of the other children watching me. I put my shoes on and he closes the front door behind us. Normally if I was walking with the Super everyone would know I was in big-big trouble, but they all know what's happened; something like that doesn't stay a secret long.

'Where are we going?' I ask.

'Let's walk down the road, shall we?'

We walk out the Homes and over the bridge and past the bus stop that I get the bus from.

'It's been a rather eventful few months for you, hasn't it, Lesley?'

'Aye, sir.'

'I just wanted to check how you were doing.'

I think about how to answer this and in the end I settle on the truth.

'I don't know how I'm doing, sir. I just want things to go back to normal.'

'That's understandable.'

'I don't know if they will ever be normal, but I keep hoping if I can get to the end of another day then mibbie the next day will be normal. They have to be normal soon, don't they?'

'One day, but I can't tell you when that day will be.'

'I hope it is soon.'

We walk along in silence for a bit near the stream; the only sound is the water finding its way around the rocks.

'Lesley, I imagine you have some questions. I might not be able to answer them all, but I'll do my best.'

I have never seen this caring side of the Super, I couldn't have imagined there was one.

'Why would Mrs Paterson do that? Why would she kill Jane because *Mr Paterson* did things to Jane years ago? And if it hadn't been for that, Sally and Jonesy wouldn't have died, right?'

Mr Gordon looks off at one of the fields, as if he is trying to work out how to best put into words something that he thinks I might not understand. I understand things; he must know this by now.

'All I can tell you is what I think, what the police think now that they have arrested Mr Paterson – he has told them some, but not all, of the story. Mr and Mrs Paterson didn't have a ... normal relationship. Because of Mrs Paterson being attacked when she was younger, she wasn't able to do things a normal husband and wife do together.'

'Like make babies?'

'Sort of like that, yes. But Mr Paterson has a sickness – he likes young girls, which is very wrong. As far as I can tell, they had an arrangement where she didn't intervene.'

'I see ...' I say, then, 'No, wait, why did Mrs Paterson kill Jane, then? Had Mr Paterson been with Jane and Mrs Paterson was jealous of her?'

'It's a bit more complicated than that. Mr Paterson ... interfered with Jane when she lived at Cottage 5 several years ago, when she was much younger. You may be aware that a teacher was recently removed from the school—'

'Mr Taylor? They say he was going with Jane.' I don't tell the Super about the diary Jonesy found. That's our secret.

'Yes ... it may be that an inappropriate relationship with her teacher brought back memories of her time at Cottage 5. Jane realised what Mr Paterson had done to her was wrong, and she told him that she was going to tell Mr Taylor.'

I remembered Jane's last diary entry, written on the day of her death: 'Meeting T tomorrow, getting things sorted.' If she'd only told Mr Taylor sooner, they'd all still be alive.

'If that happened,' the Super went on, 'Mr Paterson thought it would be reported to the authorities. He would go to jail and Mrs Paterson would have to leave the Homes. He told his wife, and Mrs Paterson killed Jane to stop her speaking out. Perhaps she thought she would not be a suspect, being a woman. I understand that Jane's body was ... posed to make it look like a man had been involved.'

I nod. I remember when Jonesy said that Jane's knickers had been round her ankles. It seems so long ago.

'And Sally? Did Mr Paterson try the same thing with her as well?'

'No, Sally was Jane's friend. Jane had told her about what Mr Paterson had done to her when she was younger. After Jane was murdered, Sally made the mistake of telling Mrs Paterson that she believed her husband had killed Jane to stop her reporting his crime. It was a fatal error – Mrs Paterson killed Sally too.'

'Ah,' I say, as if I understand it all, but I don't. It's so hard to realise that someone you thought you knew so well could do that. The person who has turned out my bedroom light all these years, helped me when I was scared, but was capable of such cruelty. I could see why Sally had thought she was safe to approach, why she might need to be warned about her husband.

Now I understand how Mr Paterson had the alibis Detective Walker explained about. He really didn't kill Sally or Jane, and Mrs Paterson probably told lies about them both being somewhere else when Jonesy was murdered. The police thought the same person killed all three girls, so they wouldn't have looked too closely at Mr Paterson by the time Jonesy died.

I wonder if Detective Walker is in trouble now, him and the other policemen. He thought alibis were so important. Did they ask for Mrs Paterson's, or did they think only the housefathers could be killers?

I am silent for a bit. I suddenly think I understand why Eldrey is gone. Why she was always so quiet. Why Mr Paterson made her come to his study for a belting so often. But I don't say it out loud. If Mr Gordon says I'm right then that would make it real, and everything is already too real. I hope they find Eldrey her own Eadie to help her.

'Mr Paterson has confessed to Morag Jones's murder,' went on Mr Gordon. 'He and Mrs Paterson were having an argument about Jane and Sally, then Morag came home during the day. She overheard them shouting in their living room. He said he had no choice.'

I remember Mrs Paterson by my hospital bed, holding my hand. I hadn't quite understood what she was saying to me at the time. About my 'little pal'. About having no choice.

'But they did. They did have a choice.'

'I know that Lesley, that's how we think, but some people think differently from us. Some people are just evil.'

'Do you think Peter Montrose made Mrs Paterson evil?'

'I don't know, Lesley, some things you can't explain.'

That phrase sticks in my head like a flag. *Some things you can't explain.*

He's still talking but I'm not listening. I like things to be explained, I like to understand them. I *need* to understand them; things need to have a reason, otherwise we are lost.

Maybe that's why grown-ups lie, because they can't explain things. Maybe they don't know the answer and don't want to seem like they don't. Is that why they have religion and God and all that business? Because there are so many things that they can't explain that they have found a reason to scoop up all the unexplainable and difficult stuff?

I realise that no one has a clue what is going on and I am going to have to get used to that if I am ever to be happy again.

The world of adults is a mess. I think when I finally get out of this place it is only going to be more of the same. But at least I am prepared.

75

A few weeks after Mrs Paterson's death I received a letter:

Dear Lesley,

The Superintendent has kept me informed of what has been going on at the Homes. I have been unable to contact you as the rules of the Homes are such that I should not be in contact with the children, particularly once I explain the reason I have left.

The Superintendent has been extremely kind in making an exception in this case, given what has happened to you. I am sure you know now what a good man he can be, and the difficult job he has to do. He doesn't often let people see his good side, but it is there – I can vouch for that.

I want you to know you are so very brave and I am so very proud of you. What you have been through is awful, but I am glad you are concentrating on your studies.

I am so sorry I had to leave the Homes suddenly.

It was never my intention to leave without saying goodbye; in fact, it was never my intention to leave, but circumstances meant that I was removed from my role.

I am six months pregnant. It is not something I intended, and I am not with the father any more. That I am unmarried and pregnant is something that the people who run the Homes consider a bad influence on you children, as so many, including yourself, were born to unmarried mothers.

I will be keeping the baby, but it means I will not be returning to work. The thing that disappoints me most about that is that I will not be able to see you again. You deserve the best, and any pain you are going through now will only go to making you into the exceptional woman I know you will become.

I want you to have the confidence to go out and make a difference in the world, because it's waiting for you.

Yours with love,
Eadie

P.S. If the baby is a girl, I am going to name her Lesley.

Postscript

The idea of this novel has been twenty-five years in the making. It started when my father suddenly died one Friday dinnertime in the gym at work. My mum was forty-seven at the time and the shock was shattering.

I was twenty-one and in the aftermath of it all I moved back home to be with her. We started to talk more than we ever had before, now that it was just me and her in the house together, and she would tell stories of her upbringing. She had grown up in the Quarriers orphan village near Bridge of Weir in Scotland. Until then I had known very little about her early life. I knew we didn't have grandparents on her side, but little else was explained.

The idea of the Quarriers homes fascinated me; that you would have one thousand children in a purpose-built village seemed so strange. My mother did not realise that most children lived with their parents until she was about six.

There is a real Morag 'Jonesy' Jones, who inspired the character in this book. She is alive and well, and is still friends with my mum to this day. During the time when Mum was trying to put her life back together after my father's death, Morag came down to stay with us and help look after her. Seeing the two of them together was fascinating: Mum went from being my mother to a teenager, and helped me see what she was like as a young woman rather than just my parent.

Mum and Jonesy didn't actually know each other whilst in the Quarriers homes, but they moved in together shortly after Mum left at sixteen and became best friends straight away. They were so different from one another but both true survivors in what was a brutal place to grow up. I was inspired to write this by their courage, brains and bravery – they overcame the rough hand life had dealt them – and I wanted it published before the generation of people who had been in these types of places was gone.

Mum went on to have three children and seven grand-children, and became an actuary as, like Lesley, she loved maths as a girl. She is now retired and living in Surrey. On the twentieth anniversary of Dad's death we went up to where we had scattered his ashes on Gleniffer Braes. Afterwards we drove to the Quarriers homes so Mum could show us where she had grown up and her 'cottage'.

After I had finished writing this book there was a development in my mother's story. She googled her own mother's name and found out that she had died a couple of months earlier. After waiting a period of time, and getting up the courage to do so, she wrote a letter to the eldest of her mother's other children, thinking that at seventy-two she didn't want to spend the rest of her life wondering *what if* she had tried to make contact with them.

They wrote back and after some confirmation of the facts my mother now has four sisters. They are in regular contact, she has met up with them, and she now has siblings for the first time in her life. They are the loveliest of people and I am so happy for my mum.

Lesley's mother in this book is completely fictional; that said, many unmarried women at the time were pressured into giving up their children by society; in fact, I have seen a handwritten letter from my grandmother to the Homes saying she only wanted her child in there for a couple of years as she wanted to be able to bring her back into the family. Although it took far longer, Mum is now back with her family.

This whole story is a tribute to my mum, who is an inspirational woman in the quietest, most dignified way. I wanted this book to show that courage comes in many forms.

This story is set in a fictional Scottish orphans' village in the 1960s. Truly awful things did happen in the real Quarriers homes. I haven't told that story here; that is for others to tell. Adults from Mum's cottage have been prosecuted and gone to prison for what they did. There were good people in the Homes trying to help the children there but there were also some very, very bad ones too.

If you were affected, there are support groups such as http://www.fbga.org.

Acknowledgements

The Montrose murders in the book are a reference to the Manuel murders, which occurred at a similar time, with a bit of artistic licence. I interviewed my mother extensively about her time at the homes. If I have got anything wrong, I apologise.

*

There are many people to thank for helping this book to publication. First is the High Priestess of Viper – Miranda Jewess, without whose help, insight, vision and this would not have got here. I would also like to thank Therese and the rest of the gang at Viper and Profile, who are utterly wonderful.

Huge thanks to Caroline Dawnay and Kat Aitken at United Agents for helping find a home for this story and for being so brilliant over the years: you are amazing.

Thank you Sheila McIlwraith, who helped hugely with an early iteration of this book, and Charlotte van Wijk, who was the first person to make me think maybe I had a story.

Thank you to the prereaders who saw an early version of this story: Simon Wort, Karen Yems, Vickie Ridley & Nik Upton – I really appreciate the help you gave.

Huge love to all the gang at Lucky's and the Saints for listening to me bore on about this book for too long.

Thank you to my mum, brother and sister, plus extended family and now new extended family. I hope to meet you all soon

Finally to Catherine, Felix, Alice and Mr B, thank you for your help, patience and for being the reason for everything. I am a lucky man to have you in my world and you make it all worthwhile.